HOW DADDY LOST HIS EAR

And Other Stories

Sallie Bingham

HOW DADDY LOST HIS EAR

And Other Stories

Sallie Bingham

TURTLE POINT PRESS
Brooklyn, New York

Requests for permissions to make copies
of any part of the work should be sent to:
Turtle Point Press, 208 Java Street, Fifth Floor, Brooklyn, NY 11222
info@turtlepointpress.com

Library of Congress Control Number: 2025943043

The author wishes to thank the following organizations
for their recognition of some the stories in the collection:

"What I Learned from Fat Annie," winner of the 2023
Thomas Wolfe Fiction Prize, North Carolina Writers' Network.

"How Daddy Lost His Ear," second prize in the 2023 Sean O'Faolain
Short Story Competition, Munster Literature Centre, Ireland.

"July Fourth," Honorable Mention in the 2024 Stories
That Need to Be Told Contest, TulipTree Publishing.

Print ISBN: 978-1-885983-22-0
eBook ISBN: 978-1-969010-00-2

Book cover and layout design by: *the*BookDesigners

First Edition
Printed in the United States of America

For J.D.V.

Who Gave Me the Seeds

CONTENTS

WHAT I LEARNED FROM FAT ANNIE

When Daddy was courting Fat Annie, she gave us a chandelier, not a cheap wire contraption but hand-forged welded iron. Daddy wouldn't haul it in from his truck along with all her bags and boxes. Said he never asked for no goddamned chandelier so my sister Nola and I went out and dragged it in.

The chandelier lay in the corner of our big room for about a month till Dad said either hang it or haul it to the dump. By that time Fat Annie had her stuff more or less corralled behind the tablecloth strung across a wire to cut off where they slept from where the rest of us, all four slept in the one big bed or on the floor. I liked the floor. With the heat from the woodstove it was warmer.

So it seemed like it was up to Nola and me to hang the chandelier. She wanted to put it in our big room but

I said it would never look right there. I don't know how I knew that but I knew. The big room was a junkpile and the chandelier was not junk. So we fetched the ladder and the chandelier to the kitchen and Nola found a piece of baling wire and we nailed that up to the ceiling beam and made a hook and hung the chandelier. It was made to hold twelve candles but we didn't have no candles and weren't likely to get any. It looked better plain than it would have outfitted with candles, so I was satisfied.

Nola not so much. She was thirteen and starting to get weird and all the time missing our mom but I was eleven and didn't miss Mom a lot. She'd gone off a long time ago with some guy, which was all Daddy told us and we knew better than to ask questions except for Linc who's only seven and he asked if she was ever coming back and got swatted across the room and she isn't even his mom. His mom is Lolana and she's already come and gone.

Daddy felt bad after that. He usually felt bad when he sobered up. He took Linc on his knee and petted him and said he was named for a great man, a president, and had a lot to live up to. Linc looked up at him and I guess he felt better.

Can't none of his women abide Daddy for long. He's rough as a cob when he's drunk and we kids know to scatter but his women always tries to argue with him. I guess if I ever want to keep a woman I can't get drunk and I've been nipping from Daddy's whiskey bottle since I was five so sober is gonna take some doing.

But this is really about Fat Annie and the second thing I want to say about her after the chandelier is she wasn't really fat. Just average with a moon face and big bazookas and a hind end to match, which was the way Daddy chose his women. She liked the baby and Linc because they was young and didn't remember their mother and she didn't bother me none but Nola took against her and wouldn't eat her food. I was always hungry and didn't see no profit in starving so when Annie was setting out the food, she and me got to talking.

That was during those long winter nights when Daddy took off for Sheridan—no liquor allowed on the rez but Sheridan is only about twenty miles west—and wasn't likely to come home till the next day. He'd sleep on the floor of the bar after closing if they'd let him or in his truck.

The first night he done that, Annie asked me if she'd drove him off. She was washing the supper dishes (she was some kind of great cook, even knew how to soften up the scrawny deer Dad sometimes brought in) and I was drying and putting away because Nola wouldn't.

When Annie asked me her question, she was at the sink and she looked at me over her shoulder and the florescent bulb made her skin pure white. I found out later she was only one-fifth Native which Dad didn't like because he's a pureblood. Us kids are all mixed anyhow. My mom and Nola's is a white girl from Arkansas that Dad met at a rodeo down there. Linc's kind of tan. The baby has a Crow mother and I guess he'll go back to live on her rez when he's a little older. So for Annie to be one-fifth Native and the rest white didn't come as any surprise to me but why she wanted Daddy, a pure Native man mean as a snake, was beyond me. I had to be growed myself before I got it.

After she asked, I saw Annie's mouth purse up like she was going to cry and I said, "He always goes to Sheridan unless there's a storm and the road's too bad."

"He did that with your mom?"

"I guess."

She was scrubbing the big pot from the stew. "Did he beat her?"

"If she went on arguing too long, he'd give her a whack and head out the door." I knew that was his way.

"Women don't understand men," Annie said, setting the pot on the drainer. We'd had beef stew and eaten every scrap, Linc begging to scrape out the burned parts and she'd let him.

I dried the pot and put it on the shelf.

"We think they want to stay with us but they don't," Annie said. "Remember what I'm saying when you're all growed up."

"Uncle Jake stays with Auntie Lenora just about all the time," I said.

"Well, he's in a wheelchair. I expect when he was young and hearty he went to Sheridan with your dad."

I didn't say nothing. I reached for another plate and started to dry it and put it away. It had a chain of red flowers around the edge.

"What I don't understand," Annie said, lowering herself into the rocker by the stove, "is why we want them to stay. All the time bitching and moaning about them going off when we know good and well they always will. More peaceful anyway once they're gone."

I put away the last plate and went and stood by the stove. I'd loaded it up good with logs and the heat felt fine. I was waiting for Annie to go on but then Linc come bitching about something and she had to go see to him and change the baby and put them both to bed and by the time she got back to the rocker it was late and she told me to go on to bed and leave her in peace.

After that we got in the way of talking just about every evening after supper when Daddy was off in his truck or out at the barn taking care of his horses. He rides saddle broncs at the rodeo and all three of his horses was broke and trained special. So we talked or Annie talked and I listened while we finished the supper dishes.

I went back to where we broke off the night before. "Don't some women run off before the men do?"

"The smart ones do," she said. "Look at your mom. I seen from her picture she was young and pretty and would do all right anywhere."

"Must be some others don't want men hanging around."

"Some so old they growed sense," she said, "and lost their appetite too."

I guessed what she meant from the groaning and hollering behind the tablecloth just about every night Daddy was home.

Annie give me a pat on the shoulder. "You'll know all about that in another two-three years. Now you just make sure you don't marry the first one."

I didn't plan to get all weird like Nola, who was putting Daddy in an uproar staying out late with Randy in his pickup. She didn't seem happy that winter, and sure enough by spring she was showing.

"There's lots of men help out," I said next evening to get Annie started. "I mean bring home wages and stuff."

"*When* there's wages," she said. "And stuff is just commodities. Beans and sugar and flour, like I'm going to spend all day baking and stewing."

"Daddy trades ours for whiskey anyways," I said.

"Now, that's sensible." She liked to drink with him at the start.

Annie lasted four years and it was only the last week that was bad. That's when she started packing her boxes and bags and when I askd her why she was going, she said Daddy told her he wanted more kids and she was too old but the truth of it is she run off with a ranger. I remembered the one time I heard Daddy and the other elders talking about how every man had to do his best to replace all the ones we lost to sickness and white killing and I knew if he was talking that way there was nothing Annie could do. He's kind of young still and sort of good-looking and he's always had lots of choices.

One night later that week when Daddy come home early from Sheridan and passed out on the floor of our big room, I watched Annie work his keys out of his jacket pocket and take off the one she needed. She got her coat and told me to help her load. On the way to Daddy's truck—it was snowing and the wind was up—she said, "Now don't you tell your Dad nothing about this 'cause he's not going to believe you and if you get a hiding you can't blame me."

By then she was in the truck and turning on the engine and starting to back out but she rolled down the window and said, "Now you remember what I told you. Don't you go marrying the first one." Then she was driving down the dirt road and I saw snow falling through the yellow of her headlights. "You keep that chandelier!" she shouted back at me.

Yes, I did get a whipping because of the truck and that was the last of many because I run off the next week. I was looking for something different and didn't even know what it was but Daddy had his new woman behind the curtain and the noise was terrible. Then Nola run off with Randy and landed somewhere east of here and so on and so on. There just don't seem to be any end to any of it that I could see.

Well, of course Daddy come after me and found me sleeping under the old railroad bridge in Sheridan—that was how far I got—and would have beat me again but I was near as big as he was and he knew I could give him as good as I got.

"What in hell you trying to do?" he shouted. "Don't I treat you good, plenty of food and now with Ruby she's some kind of a cook and you're living high on the hog?"

"I don't want food, I want my mom," I said and old as I was I started to blubber. Never had thought of her before.

"She's working in a house in Denver, I'll take you to meet her," he said and I remembered what Fat Annie had told me about her being still young and pretty.

That started me to blubbering again and the old son of a bitch put his arm around me and herded me to his truck just like a little sheep.

Next week he told me to pack some clean socks and we drove up through the mountains to Denver. The pass was thick with snow (they closed it next day) but Daddy knew snow and the way he spurred that old truck through the drifts had me nearly surprised.

We got into Denver about nightfall and went to a place he knew that took people like us. It wasn't too bad, the bed they give us was big and didn't have no bugs in it. I got in and went to sleep and Daddy hit the bars and didn't get back till daylight and then had to sleep it off.

I walked around the city and saw all the sights and the big roads packed with traffic till I got so cold I had to go back to the place.

Daddy was up and he said we was going to meet my mom and we started out walking. The place she was at was in another part of town, a nice-looking house with a brass door knocker.

The lady who let us in told us to wait on a bench in the front hall. Men came and went, stumbling over our feet and Daddy said hello to each of them as if he'd known them forever. Natives and black and white, he seemed to know them all.

Mom came downstairs. I didn't know it was Mom till Dad stood up and cuffed her and kissed her and said, "I brung your son, run off last week looking for you or so he said."

Mom was pretty as Fat Annie told me, blond long hair hanging down over her shoulders and a little pointy nose and a firmed-up mouth like a rose. She led Dad into the parlor and sat him in a big rocker and got on his lap and they rocked and giggled like a couple of kids.

"Your boy's all growed up," he said after a while and she looked at me and didn't know me and I didn't know her either.

"Hello, son," she said.

"Hello," I said.

Then she asked Daddy if he'd brought me to be plucked but he said he didn't have the time. She said it wouldn't take more than twenty minutes but Daddy wasn't buying.

"Well, now you've seen her," Daddy said, herding me to the door. "Are you satisfied?"

"Goodbye, be good!" she called.

Daddy didn't expect an answer and I didn't give him one and that was the first and last time I saw my mom.

After that I didn't have nothing to say about nothing. Ruby was a good cook although nothing compared to Fat Annie and I went back to drying the dishes. I thought it was going to go on and on that way but lo and behold it didn't.

The spring I turned sixteen I was helping Daddy at the rodeo down in Albuquerque, cleaning his tack and feeding his horses and so on and one evening when I was finishing up the chores this girl come walking by and stopped to talk.

I'm not going to say nothing about Missy McKinley because the way I feel about her ain't nobody's business. She come from Denver, was down our way just out of pure curiosity—nobody in her family rodeo'd and she'd never been to one before. We ended up talking every night of the five-day event and she introduced me to her brother who'd driven her and the next day I got in the back seat of his Ram and rode to Denver with the two of them and started in at her high school and found out I could do more than just barely read and write.

I heard Daddy found out where I was but by then he'd given up on me and didn't cause me no trouble.

I sleep in the loft at Missy McKinley's family house and eat with them and earn my way doing anything they need doing. Missy and I sit in the kitchen and talk most evenings and I never have touched her though that time is coming and we both know it. She was my first and she was also my best but I did think twice about what Fat Annie told me. I never did marry Missy McKinley though we took up living together.

Things changed of course and after two years Missy McKinley turned on me and said it was all nothing but work and no fun and I was gone too much. I did tell her she never had sprouted no seed of mine. I'd hooked a good job, foreman on a rig in the oil patch down south, and didn't get home till the weekend and it was a long drive and some Saturdays I just couldn't make it. The money was good and I'd bought us a nice new trailer home but it seemed like it didn't do no good.

I tried to jolly her, telling her maybe she wanted

a real nice chandelier for our kitchen—I'd seen one at Sears—but she swatted me across the face and that was the end of it as far as I was concerned.

She run off to Denver to live with her folks again. They never had anything good to say about me, called me "that damn cowboy."

So I guess you could say I did learn something from Fat Annie but what I learned was when to let the woman call it quits.

Missy McKinley took my pickup but I give her the keys so no hard feelings because she was my first and she was also my best.

HOW DADDY LOST HIS EAR

"They was fighting," my cousin Tara tells me. She's the only person I've ever known named for a house. They went down to Georgia one time to find it but didn't. Tore down a long time before.

"They wasn't fighting," I tell her. "Mama Blacksleeves took the truck and got stuck in the mud a yard from the house. Daddy was trying to help her get out."

"Those Blacksleeves always getting themselves into pickles," Tara says. We're sitting on the porch of our old house—this was years after it happened—and Tara being as nice as she is brought out some store-bought lemonade, too sweet for me but let that pass. Ever since my days at the Jesuit boarding school in Helena I've stayed off sweets and it wasn't something they told me, just instinct. I aim to stay strong.

At the time of this talk I was twenty-four, Tara a year younger. We're both breeds with white mamas gone since early. I take after Daddy, dark with the same long shiny hair I wear mostly braided. Tara's pretty like her mama, a Salt Lake City girl didn't care for the rez. I never expected Tara to stick around either but she found herself a boyfriend—Joe Pinchbelly, a Crow. We don't hold with that tribe but nothing was going to stop Tara once she fixed on him, visited him regular for two years at the prison down in Deer Lodge and married him soon as he got out. He's off working the oil patch now and so she come back home for company.

"So what happened?" Tara asks me, digging a loose cigarette out of her jeans pocket. She takes a while getting it to light with her pretty pink lighter.

I tell her, "Daddy got behind the truck to push and told Mama to rock it back and forth to get out of the mud hole. I was in the house, heard him shouting at her. She had the tires screaming, digging down deeper in the mud every time she stepped on the gas. Daddy was hollering at her to stop but I guess she didn't hear him 'cause she went right on trying to rock the truck. Flew back and knocked Daddy flat."

"Well, she didn't kill him," Tara says, not too fond of old Daddy—he always grabbing at her. "Caught him with the edge of the bumper and drove over his ear."

"How'd she do that?"

"The only part of him was under the tire."

She starts to laugh. I tell her to shut up. "You wouldn't of been laughing if you'd seen the blood. Bled like a stuck pig. I ran him on in the house, found some rags, bound up his head."

"What about his ear?"

"Put it in a plastic bag, throwed it in the freezer. Got it out when I drove him down to the IHS. They sewed it on, but crooked."

"How in the world!"

"I don't know but crooked it was and crooked it stayed. Why he always wears his cap pulled low."

"Yeah, but I saw that ear one time when he was coming out of the shower. Crooked as hell! Was he mad. 'Nothing for you to stare at you little...'" She stops.

We both take a minute to look out over our field that's full of downed cornstalks left from our last harvest five years before. After that with the drought we give up on that field, all the good gone out of it once the spring dried up.

"What happened to Mama Blacksleeves?" Tara asks.

"She got out of the mud hole some way, drove on off, never did come back."

"Smart. Did your Daddy go after her?"

"No. Said good riddance. They didn't get on too well after the first month."

She nods. "He was still missing your mama."

"I doubt it."

"He always said she was prettier than anything else come down the pike."

"Pretty don't count much in the long run. She was always after him—do this, do that. A man can't hardly stand that kind of woman."

"Not if she's right," Tara says with the smirk that used to make me want to hit her. "Here he comes now."

Daddy hit the cattle guard so hard coming through the gate we could hear it all the way to the porch.

I don't know what it is about Daddy but we both stand up when he comes, toting a bag of booze.

"You two go on in and clean up that kitchen," he tells us. "Godawful mess from last night." Hawk and them had come over and we did party considerable.

We go in like he tells us, always have and always will, I guess. Tara fills a bucket and gets the mop—"Whew this thing stinks!"—and starts on the floor. I pick up dishes and stack them in the sink while Daddy unbags his booze and gets started with a few sips straight from the bottle. Tara fetches him a glass. He backhands it off the kitchen table and we watch it skitter across the linoleum.

"When is that man of yours going to come back and make me some babies?" he asks her.

"I'm not looking to make any babies for you, old man." She can be fresh.

Daddy reaches to grab her but she hops out of the way.

"You with that crooked ear!"

He grabs his hat, which he's taken off coming in, and slaps it back on. "You want to stay in my house, eat my food, you watch your tongue, bitch," he says.

"What food there is."

It's heating up. "I was telling how Mama Blacksleeves run over your ear," I says.

He starts laughing. He can do that anytime. "She tried to tell me she was sorry!"

"I thought she hightailed it out of here."

"Did, but there's still the phone."

"Well, she did the right thing leaving," Tara says, pious as a church.

"You think I give a shit about that?" Now he's smooth, shiny, the way he can always get. "There's one thing a woman can do for me and one thing only and when she quits on that, I quit on her."

I've heard this story about a hundred times. "Why don't you go on in to the IHS, let them knock you out, take that ear off, and sew it on straight?" I ask.

"I'm finished with that place. Last time I went they tried to stick that ass camera up me. Quit when I screamed. Like being fucked by a gorilla."

And there the three of us are, laughing when there isn't a thing in the world to laugh about. But that's Daddy. There's people who hold things together and it's never the people you think it ought to be. Uncle Joe worked years at the sawmill, only drunk on Saturday nights, had a white wife from Oklahoma, five half-white kids, but he never could hold anything together, while Daddy with his storming keeps the two of us in his house when we should have been long gone. Maybe waiting to see when his next shouting will happen, who will get slapped sideways, or maybe even waiting for the day he quits storming and starts acting like he cares, a day we both know never will come. But meantime he can always get us laughing.

Now he stops laughing first. "I'm peckish," he says with that lip curl we know means get something on the table fast. Tara goes in the kitchen, opens the freezer, digs out some buffalo burgers. Daddy always demands meat. She throws the patties in leftover pan grease in the skillet and Daddy and I go in the kitchen to watch the fat jump and spatter. I get out plates and forks—Tara makes me wash them, they was put away half dirty—and just when she's forking out those burgers we hear tires in the yard.

Daddy looks out the window and then I see his small smile. "Well, look who's coming."

Tara keeps on putting out the meat but I go to the window and there's Daddy's red Ford truck parking by the stump. Mama Blacksleeves rolls out.

"You want her in here?" I ask Daddy but he's already throwing open the screen door and holding his arms out like they've been empty since she left three months before, which they have not.

Mama Blacksleeves runs up on the porch and then he has her grabbed up tight against his chest and they're both bawling. "Oh, I missed you, honey," Daddy says.

"How come you never called me?" she asks, black eye makeup tracking down her face with her tears.

Daddy never answers questions and so we don't know why he never called this woman he's grabbing so tight.

"Knew you'd come home when you was ready," he tells her, voice all gummed up with tears.

"Well I'm here now," she says, smearing her face with the back of her hand. "Tell your boy to get my stuff out of the truck."

I was already out the door and down the steps but then I had to holler back for the keys. Can you believe she'd locked Daddy's truck? She digs the keys out of her bag and throws them to me and then she and Daddy watch me unload a ton of her stuff, three green garbage bags full to bursting, two suitcases, and some cardboard boxes.

"Where you want it?" I ask Daddy but she answers, smooth as silk, "Our bedroom, Sure Enough, thought you knew by now." They still call me that, claiming when I was little I said it all the time.

When I come back, Tara has the buffalo burgers served up with slices of paper towel for napkins and

Daddy's special hot sauce and we all sit down and eat. I start to ask Mama Blacksleeves why she's come back but Tara gives me one of her looks. Daddy is talking about bringing in a bunch of cowboys to herd the mama cows up to the hill country for the summer and I want to say he won't need no cowboys because our old herd was sold off when the drought took the grass and the two we have left for old times sake I can bring up without any trouble. I can do it myself but don't offer because Daddy says a man who offers before he's asked is a fool.

Tara drives off to her nurse class at the community college and Daddy and Mama go to their room and I shut my ears as best I can and start wrangling dirty dishes. When I've done as much as I aim to do I go out on the porch to smoke and look off toward the Kootenai, where the trees are just leafing up. I might have closed my eyes for a minute and when I open them, here come Daddy and Mama grinning like a pair of cats.

"I guess you're back to stay a while," I say to Mama, a little bit more peeved than I have any right to be. She's not my mother, never has tried to boss me.

"Oh, for a while anyway," she says. "I'm aiming to go to L.A. in the fall."

Daddy gives the hanging flesh on her upper arm a good pinch. "What's there we ain't got here, darlin'?"

"Everything," she says, and she reaches up and traces that crooked ear with her finger. Daddy tries to swat off her hand but she won't let him and it seems to me I'm seeing something I've never seen before: Daddy smiling. Not grinning. Smiling the way you see a old dog smile when you give him a bone and I know Mama Blacksleeves is here to stay, at least till fall.

Late that afternoon when Tara comes back I tell her my thought but she don't believe me 'cause women never stay here except for her.

That evening Mama Blacksleeves and Daddy go down to Sheridan and won't be back till the bars close at two a.m. so Tara and I get settled comfortable, me in my sleeping bag on the floor and her on the bed. I never dispute that with her. Being a girl, she needs a bed with a sheet and a door with a lock while for me it's "immaterial"—that's a word I picked up somewhere and use pretty regular when things are heating up. I never have been one to fight about nothing and I like Tara and wish sometimes she weren't my cousin. I like her breasts, not big but shapely and she has no trouble showing them off in her thin shirts.

Daddy comes roaring and stomping in at some dark hour with Mama Blacksleeves trying to shush him. They step around me like I'm a log in the road, go in the kitchen and pull this and that out of the refrigerator. Daddy always comes back hungry from the bars.

He's cursing because all he can find is an old brown banana, some cheese, and yogurt gone bad but Mama gets him to shut up and they trundle off to bed. After that things are pretty quiet till cockcrow, when it all gets started again.

Daddy is going to drive down to the Burger King "before I starve to death" and we go with him and Mama, not that he's asked—he never asks—but we just know to go along, have gone along since we was big enough to walk. Used to be the whole bunch of us, just Tara and me now but before it was my big brother Pat (he's over in Iran) and Clinker who got shot dead in a bar fight a few years back and Norma who's married to a white man and gone. We was one big bunch then herded into the red truck to go somewhere, anywhere, with Daddy and he'd curse and say he never counted on no bunch of snotty-nosed kids but when we got to wherever he was going, he made us get out and introduced us to everybody there. Bar, hardware store, feed store, fast food, it don't matter, he has friends everywhere and he wanted them to know he had this bunch of kids. When we was little we'd be picking our noses or shuffling our bare feet in the dirt but one look from him and we'd straighten up and "fly right," hands at our sides and feet still and quiet. Now with just the two of us I wonder if he's going to do the same thing.

Well, it turns out he's going to the cemetery and I don't remember ever going there except when somebody was getting buried like Clinker. He stops the truck by the fence and we climb out after him and follow him like little sheep through the gate. He heads to the far corner and Tara says, "He's been here before, he knows where he's going," and I have to say yes though I can't hardly imagine it. Next thing she'll have him coming with flowers.

Strides across to the far corner with us trailing after him and drops on his knees by this wooden cross. Tara pushes on my shoulder and I get down beside him and from there I can see the name.

Missy McKinley

Blessed Are The Pure In Heart

Mama Blacksleeves is getting down behind me, whispering to Tara, "Now, who in the name?" but Daddy turns around and gives her a look and Tara knows better than to answer.

Anyway I don't expect she knows.

Daddy uses his sleeve to wipe some dirt off the cross. "Only white woman I ever loved," he says.

"I'm amazed to hear you say it," Mama Blacksleeves tells him, and he leans back and gives her a swat. "None of your business, woman."

She's knocked back on her heels but rights herself and come out with "Well, it was years before you and me met up."

Daddy is crossing himself and mumbling prayers, raised like all of us by the Jesuits. I doubt he remembers all the mumbo jumbo but this he has down cold.

"Dust to dust, ashes to ashes, darlin'," he says. "I'll be with you before you know it."

"Thought you was going to be buried up at the rez with Grandpa Jake Bear," I say without thinking, and then I get the back of his hand.

"You'll put me in the ground next to Missy!" he shouts, and only Mama Blacksleeves is nuts enough to keep on arguing.

"You promised you'd go in the ground with me!" she shouts, and he reaches back and rolls her.

Then we're all crying and pleading. "Shut up!" Daddy says, and gets up off his knees and starts to the truck. "You're coming, come," he shouts over his shoulder, and we're scrambling, knowing he'll leave us and it's a twelve-mile walk home.

It doesn't end that way because Daddy is hungry again and so he drives to Burger King and treats us to Whoppers and milkshakes, whatever flavor we want, and by the time we get back in the truck, everything is peaceful.

Till the next day. Mama Blacksleeves still feels like she's new (second time around) and that's when Daddy's women always go too far. After a few weeks they know they're old for him—second time around, third time around, it don't matter, they wear out on him fast.

Mama don't even have sense enough to wait till Daddy's had his coffee. She looks a mess, hair all tangled up from the night and every line in her face clear as graph paper in the morning light, no lipstick nor nothing, but she starts right in.

"You know none of us is getting any younger," she says.

He grunts, wedging his right foot in his boot, getting ready to go.

"It's time we made plans," she says.

He wedges his left foot in his boot. "You always talk plans and you know I don't live my life that way." He stands up and stamps his feet down, his boots always too small and I know we're going to have a time getting them off end of the working day.

"Yeah but one of us could die anytime," Mama goes on, and I know she's been practicing this, it comes out so calm and smooth, but a little hitch at the back of her throat tells me she's going to cry. I want to tell her, *Don't cry, Daddy hates women's tears* and I only remember one of them way back, a skinny girl, telling him when he said that, "Then don't make us cry." She was gone in twenty minutes.

He's heading out the door and Mama throws her last words over his head like a rope. "I'm going in town later sign my new will. I got some property," she says.

Daddy turns back. "I don't want to hear about no 'property,'" he says. "I got twelve hundred and twenty acres here, more than I need or want."

"Yeah but I got mining rights on mine," she says, just about purring. Daddy never has been able to get a hold of the mining rights for his land—some rich cat from Denver bought them a long time ago before Old Jake Bear knew what was going on.

She's caught his attention now and he hangs in the doorway watching her. "You planning on starting in the mining business?"

"Could be," she says. "My daddy sold our rights on the mountain ranch to Colorado Old Mining made a bunch of money. I might do the same with the valley place."

"And tore up your ranch so nobody don't live there no more."

"What are you, one of them conservanists?"

He reaches to swat her but she ducks. "Never knew you to care about tearing up the land," she says, pleased as a kid with a candy bar.

"You'll come whining when they tear down your old house in the valley to get at what's under it," he says.

"It's going to be a lot of money, enough to build a big new house and then some."

She's riled him to where he's going to ask a question and that takes some doing. "You got plans for me too?"

She grins. "Maybe. Sit down and let's talk about it."

"I got to feed the horses," he says, out the door before she can stop him but I know it's not the end. She has that wild blind look in her eye like a horse heading to the barn and ain't nothing going to stop her.

"Let him eat before you start in," I tell her, but she never has listened to me and don't begin now. So as soon as Daddy comes in the door at five, covered with the day's dirt and heading for the shower, she puts herself in his way and starts. "We get married I'll put you in my will," she says.

"I'll die first," he tells her, and I hear from his tone he's been calculating.

"You let me start taking care of you, you'll outlive us all."

"So what's my side of this bargain?" he asks her, and I kind of admire the way she's pushed him this far.

"Just be nice to me," she says. She's been thinking this out for a while. "I don't count on you being faithful," she tells him with that hitch in the back of her throat.

"Not faithful but loyal," he says, and I try to remember how many times I've heard him say that. I don't know why but with these women it never seems to get old.

"You'll want some girl and that's OK with me but you'll always come back," she says, making it not a wish but a promise.

"I'll think on it," he says, and I'm amazed. He pulls off his shirt heading for the shower, and I see his old-man belly and the white hair on his chest.

I hear them disputing long into the night but they're in bed covered up to the eyes and I can't make out the words. Only he's not shouting and cursing and she's going on and on like a shallow stream bumping over rocks but still going.

I get to sleep before they do and in the morning I see her shaking out the blanket and smiling and I wonder what they agreed to if they agreed to anything and is this going to change my life.

Daddy is out early seeing to the well—it's running dry and if it does we'll be finished here. I hear the pump groaning when it hits mud at the bottom and Daddy tells me to haul water from the cistern and pour it in the well and I do that all morning till the pump starts to work smooth. It's not a cure but it'll get us through the day with enough water for the horses and for the little bit of cooking Mama Blacksleeves might do and maybe there'll be rain soon and the well will fill. It's happened before but now we're into something different and the sun has that glare in it means no cloud is going to hinder it anytime soon and it's way too hot for this early in the spring.

I don't know if it's the white hair on Daddy's chest or the big old-man belly pushing on his belt but they do come out of it with something they can both put their names to—Daddy making his X—and Mama Blacksleeves is so pleased she goes around the kitchen putting something together for us and singing one of her old songs. Daddy shouts at her to stop the caterwauling and she laughs and lets it go 'cause now she has what she wants or nearly.

It turns out they got to have two witnesses to get it done legal at the justice up in Fargo so Tara and I ride in the back seat of the pickup for the long drive and nobody says a word the whole way like the whole thing would tumble down with just one word as a push. I know Daddy is in a foul mood 'cause he don't even light up and I never been on a long ride with him not smoking and Mama Blacksleeves has the sense this time to say nothing. She's dolled herself up with the curling iron and enough makeup to paint a fence and somehow or other I start to feel sorry for her.

It's late afternoon by the time we get to the justice's office and he's just locking up and not pleased to have to open but Mama Blacksleeves don't give him no option and for once Daddy lets her take the lead.

The two of them stand up in front of the justice and he reads whatever from his book and I wonder why he's still got to read the words then remember nobody gets married around here so he's had no practice. Live together, yes, make some babies and then go off when it don't work.

The justice reads the words wrinkling up his nose like he smells something bad and I think he must of heard tales about Daddy but it don't matter now till he gets to the end and says, "Kiss the bride" and Daddy hollers, "What the hell!" and Mama Blacksleeves touches his arm and somehow lets him know it's OK to skip the kissing.

She shells out some bills to the justice and he gets to the door and holds it open for us to go through and I say to Tara, "I never thought to see the day."

"He's a old man now," she tells me. "Only reason it happened."

I want to think he maybe feels something about Mama Blacksleeves like now they'll be old together and can take care of each other when the time comes and won't have to go to the old people's home. I hold on to that for a while, six months maybe, till Daddy comes home drunk and she says something to him and he smashes her jaw with his fist.

I drive her down to the IHS thinking she'll cry and blab the whole way but she never says nothing, never sheds a tear, and that's when I know whatever bargain she's made with Daddy is going to stick, because he never could stand women's tears.

Then the first check comes from Colorado Old Mining and they go out to celebrate, dressed up and ready for the white people staring at them at the Ranch King, where we never go ordinarily. It costs too much but with the check in Mama Blacksleeves's hand that ain't a problem and never is going to be.

They get back and Mama decrees they're going to live in her house other side of the rez and leave this wreck to Tara and me.

Tara says she's glad of a little peace and quiet but I

miss the racket, the sex and the fighting, and it seems like the days have got longer and the nights too and I start getting ready to leave home and go somewhere, maybe Denver where I hear they're building night and day and I can get a job in construction.

I go back for their Silver or whatever—Mama Black-leeves says they don't have time to count it off in years so she turns the years into months and that way it looks like they'll get to Gold and she'll have Daddy in a suit for a big celebration.

Tara always says it's Daddy getting old that did it but I think it's when his ear got tore off and sewed back on crooked.

BEAR SKIN

I was so mad when I saw what my grandpa Old Jake Bear was doing I shouted loud as I could, "You stop!"

He didn't. Just went right on wrapping my big cousin Ed up tight in that old buffalo-skin robe, Ed passed out so he couldn't fight. Fifteen years old and big and strong—not big and strong enough to handle Grandpa.

Ed had taken to coming home late again and drunk again and Grandpa told him, "Pull yourself up, boy, you going too far"—hard to take from Old Bear 'cause he put down a half bottle of rye whiskey every night but never passed out and always slept in the bed like a Christian. Whereas my cousin Ed drank a lot of I don't what, passed out pretty regular, coming home from the bars in Sheridan in the dark of the night and falling down on the big room floor where we had to step over him to get to the bathroom.

Daddy Cowboy went on a bender just about every Saturday but stayed sober enough during the week to hold on to his job running the front loader at the Bristlecone Copper Mine that keeps everybody here on the rez going. That's why we run off those conservation ladies when they showed up two years ago to picket the mine. It's all we got and if it poisons our stream every now and then what to do about it is our say-so.

Daddy Cowboy went off to some war when I was still in diapers and Ed just starting to walk. That's what we do, go when the nation calls us though it's not our nation never was and never will be but we're warriors or used to be. That's one of the things I can't get nobody around here to talk about. Daddy Cowboy never told us nothing about what happened over there but I had the feeling he'd killed somebody or maybe more than one. Come back with a shadow over him, Mama said.

So back to big Cousin Ed. We growed up always together till he got to being a teenager and said he didn't want to run around with some fat kid.

I ain't fat like the ladies around here. Grandma Blacksleeves they had to take up to the cattle scale in Bristol and she come out at the number we expect from a two-year-old heifer. We know it's pop, beer, chips, and candy but what good does knowing do? In this life you got to have something to look forward to.

So anyway back to Ed. Once Grandpa got him

wrapped up in that old buffalo skin he sealed it with mailing tape and that's when I blew my top. "Grandpa! He'll suffocate!"

"Plenty room at the top to breathe, the little bastard."

I commenced to tear open the top to give Ed more breathing room and when I saw that long red hair of him I remembered when he used to let me braid it, and I just sat down and cried. I know there's worse things in life but I have yet to run into one hurts more than my big Cousin Ed chasing me off when I was fixing to braid his hair.

I was sitting there bawling till I felt something hard butting my ribs. Grandpa was pushing the muzzle of his pistol there and when I went to shove it off he said, "Take it and shoot him now. Same thing as turning him loose."

"The hell!" I screeched.

He slapped his palm over my mouth and I knew better than to bite him.

"Cut him loose now he'll go right back to the bars in Sheridan. Not today but tomorrow or certainly Saturday night he'll get hit by a car trying to hitch back here, thrown in the ditch and left for dead. That what you want for him?"

Which brought me to bawling again.

"Your Uncle Joe hit by a drunk driver too drunk himself to get out of the way. Your Grandma Blacksleeves sick with liver trouble from drinking. Your cousin one-time-removed Arnold blowing his nose with that cocaine. So cut Ed loose, girl, but don't come whining to me when you're getting fixed up for his funeral." It's true for us a funeral is a celebration. Well, we're Christian or most of us and it gets to the point where those pearly gates look pretty good.

"And quit that bawling," Grandpa said.

I quit, wiped my face on my sleeve, and went to sit down and wait for Ed to come to. Which he did in about an hour, fighting that bear skin like a tiger rolled up in a rug, hollering and cursing till Grandpa showed up and cut the tapes and Ed rose up out of there like a thundercloud. When he saw Grandpa standing there with his big knife the heat kind of went out of him and he looked like he was going to cry.

"Don't pull that tear stuff with me, pussy," Grandpa told him.

That brought on the tears and the kicking—everybody in the family kicks when they tear up, I used to think it was to hold the tears back but now I ain't so sure.

"Get down to the barn. I need help with that new colt," Grandpa Bear told him, and turned and walked off before I could say I'd do the job. I'm just as good as Ed if not better with horses but the men around here can't see that. Daddy Cowboy put me up bareback when I was two or so I've been told, never let me use a saddle till I could hang on with my legs and no grabbing the mane. I must of fallen a few times and if I'd had a mama around she'd have put a stop to it but my mama was long gone to the Cities and Grandma Blacksleeves weren't no use at all once she hit the bottle.

So Ed went on down to the barn and I followed along meek as milk and he didn't have enough juice left in him to curse me out for tailing him.

Grandpa was leading the new colt out of the barn. He bought him a few days back from some cowboy at the rodeo in Sheridan for next to nothing because this colt never been broke and there was some said he never would be with that mean flash in his eye.

Grandpa looped the lead rope around the colt's neck and handed the end to Ed and turned and went on back to the house like it was no difference to him what happened.

I expect Ed was counting on some help but it looked like he was going to have to get the job done on his own and I swear he looked at me like I could maybe do something but I just stuck my boot on the bottom rail of the arena and leaned on the top to watch. I didn't plan on being run off that day.

He got a saddle on the thing with it bucking and trying to tear around. One thing I'll say about my cousin, he is fearless.

He turned to lead it into the arena but that beast run up on him and bit him in the butt, a real solid mouthful of jeans and meat. Ed don't wear no underpants.

Ed never squealed nor nothing, just turned and hit that colt across the eyes with the end of the lead rope.

Thing rared up on his hind legs and tried to strike Ed but my cousin was too quick for him, jumped out of the way then hit him across the eyes with the lead till water ran.

While the colt was gathering himself for some more mischief Ed jumped from the ground and got astride before the beast knowed what was what.

He knew soon enough and commenced to buck three feet in the air, bunched up till the saddle horn stood clear. Spine bent in a curlicue, popping up and kicking to cast off the best rider alive but Ed hung on with his legs clamped like scissor blades and his spurs stuck deep in the thing's sides.

So bucking didn't work and the thing started to careen around the arena bucking and farting like a cannon and Ed hung on and used his right hand to tighten the lead rope around the thing's neck till blood and mucus ran out of its nose.

Then it all stopped and the colt stood still, shaking, head down, and Ed slid off easy and give it one pat on the neck and led it to the barn and the colt followed. Went in the stall and commenced to crunch the handful of grain Ed scooped for him.

"Seems like he's some kind of grateful," I said when Ed was rubbing him down.

"If he's smart he'll want to learn," Ed said. "If he's dumb he's no use."

I guess the colt was smart 'cause we kept him. Dumb would have gone to the knacker. Grandpa always said he don' t pay good money to feed stupid animals.

I watched Ed work that animal every day that summer. He'd get up early before the worst of the heat, put the colt through his paces till the thing knew the meaning of just the touch of one spur. I didn't think Grandpa Bear even noticed—he was off to the casino most days—but it turned out he did. Or I think he did. I never know with these men.

Around the end of the last week in August when it was starting to cool down a little Grandpa drove in pulling the trailer with a racket going on inside. Whatever he was hauling was kicking up a storm, striking the metal sides of the trailer it sounded like with all four hooves. Grandpa got out cool as a cucumber, opened the tailgate, and this fury flew out and ran six times around the arena bucking and charging and changing direction in a whirl of dust. When it had finally run itself out and stood panting, Grandpa handed the lead rope to Ed and said "Do it," turned on his heel, and walked away.

Ed looked under the thing. "A girl horse, meaner than hell."

Then before he could loop the lead rope around her neck she backed him up against the railing and pressed him so hard he had to drop to the ground to get under her. He stood up so close to that animal I thought she was going to stomp him but he jumped up on her back facing the wrong way and grabbed the stump of her tail and careened around the arena, hollering and waving his hat. The hands standing around started to yell and cheer and wherever Grandpa had got to, he must of heard the commotion and maybe remembered Ed was now the only likely male left in the family and breaking that girl horse was proof he could run the ranch when the time come.

It might have happened that way except for the fact that Grandpa outlived Ed. It seemed like my big cousin never could be satisfied. He kept on traveling all over, looking for horses nobody could ride, horses so ornery the owner was set to call the knacker and shoot the thing in the head. Ed always heard when something like that was going to happen and got there in time to grab the horse and put some bills in the owner's hand, I don't know how much, though I suspicion the owner would have given the thing away for free just to get rid of it. And then Ed would commence to work on it.

He got so good, word went out around the county and horse people started to call him to come and take some brute. Too much business for one man who wanted time off to go to the bars, so he brought on a kid and trained him up and that boy did pretty good. I knowed I could have done the same or better but no use asking Ed why he didn't choose me.

Everything was going along till Pickle got in the game. Pickle is a Crow and ordinarily we steer clear of those people (going back a long way) but when Pickle went on the rodeo circuit and commenced winning the silver buckles Daddy Cowboy used to rake in in his younger days, Ed got curious and went to watch him train.

Well, that boy had a different way of going about it. He didn't take on the monster horses, that was Ed's specialty, but the colts he chose had vinegar enough. The day Ed and I went over to the Rocking L to watch him, Pickle was working this colt that was running around the arena and I thought to see Pickle chase him. That can go on for a long time. But Pickle just held out a big carrot and that colt skidded to a stop and come to him. Then when he wanted the colt to go in the barn instead of jerking him with the lead rope Pickle just opened the gate and the colt followed him through. "Always work with what's good in a horse," he told Ed, who was leaning on the fence watching.

"What if there ain't no good?" Ed asked.

"I never met a horse yet don't have a speck of good somewhere," Pickle said, giving the colt a handful of grain before turning him loose in the paddock.

"That all you're going to do?" Ed said.

"All for today," Pickle said. "It don't do no good to wear them out. I'll saddle him tomorrow."

"I bet you will," Ed said, and went right back to doing things his way and the ranchers being what they are generally preferred him. Something sissified about the way Pickle done it, though when he started winning all those silver buckles they didn't really know what to say.

Ed went on training for a while and then it seemed like he lost interest and went to cars. He knew everything there is to know about governing horses, but cars is a different thing and a week after he got that secondhand Mazda he was ticketed for speeding and tore the ticket up and stamped it under his boot. Tribal officer knew better than to say anything—just turned and walked away.

Next thing the phone rang in the late hours of the night and woke Grandpa Bear and I heard him say, all groggy, "I don't have no grandson." I grabbed the phone and heard Ed was in the ICU in Sheridan after a bad car smash-up.

"I need you to take me to the hospital," I told Grandpa; he was laying back on the bed. "Ed's hurt bad."

"When you going to learn to drive, girl?" he said but he pulled on jeans and boots—didn't bother with no shirt, it was nighttime—and we got in his pickup and he drove like we was on the way to a picnic, slow and singing along with the late-night radio.

It wasn't no picnic at the hospital. Grandpa stuck to his story, acted like he didn't know why we was there, and sat downstairs all mad while I went in to see my cousin. He was strapped up to all kinds of machinery blinking away, his head bandaged so only his eyes was looking out. I couldn't tell whether his eyes saw me—they was kind of white and staring—and after about six minutes bells started to ring and nurses rushed in and made me go.

I sat in that waiting room the rest of the night, Grandpa grunting and snoring in a nearby chair. When the sun come, he raised up. "Let's us go and get us some coffee," he said and jerked me by the arm but I said I wasn't going nowhere with Ed that bad off and after cursing and carrying on for a while Grandpa left, telling me I'd have to find my own ride home. Which was fine by me.

People, doctors and nurses and such, were going in and out of Ed's room but I couldn't get no information and when I tried to go in and see my cousin some big nurse woman blocked me saying it was touch and go and no visitors allowed till he "stabilized." I heard the if in her voice and said I'd wait right there till somebody let me see him.

When I did finally see him, Ed was dead. The big nurse pulled the sheet up over his face but soon as her back was turned I pulled it down and there he was, his mouth all stiff and angry like death had interrupted something he really needed to say. I kneeled down right there and said a prayer, asked for blessing on my cousin so he wouldn't get stuck in purgatory—how was he going to stand that?—and then big nurse come back with papers for me to sign as next of kin. I was as close to that as anybody.

Ed never was listed as a member of our tribe—mama from elsewhere, daddy so long gone nobody remembered what he was—and so no traditional burial, just the funeral parlor in Sheridan and a sort of big cup for his ashes. Funeral man handed it to me 'cause there weren't nobody else. Grandpa kept on saying he didn't rightly know who'd died and the rest of the family took after him so nobody but me went and Grandma Blacksleeves, who was taking the week off from the bottle.

I'd chosen this cup from the book they showed me at the funeral parlor, a gold "receptacle" that looked just like the real thing till you stood it in the sun. Then it flashed and blinked like a thousand stoplights and Grandma Blacksleeves told me that was a sure sign of a fake. I didn't like to close what was left of Ed up in something not real, but what could I do? So we emptied him in the cup and put it in the ground in the new graveyard and Grandma did sing some kind of old song to bless him going.

This person none of us expected come to the graveyard and sobbed loud all the way through, black head to foot which we don't do. I asked her name but she was sobbing so hard she couldn't speak. When it was over she told me her name was Lily Jefferson and she had two kids from Ed but didn't bring them out of respect for our sorrow.

Then I knew the story was not ended but just beginning and who was going to see to those kids? Because Lily was working at the Family Dollar and her mother who was watching the kids had a growth in her belly and was going to be operated on and maybe die. I weren't in school or working, so who else?

I didn't wait to be asked. They was my big cousin's kids. I just went on over to Lily's trailer in the park at Sheridan, place fixed up real nice, trees, flowers in pots, and knocked on the screen. This old woman come out, Lily's mother not yet gone under the knife, and looked at me with all that suspicion but after I told her how I was related she let me in. It was hot in that small space and the two kids was laying on the floor looking at the TV.

"No school?" I asked the grandma, but she said they got picked on for being Native and she was fixing to homeschool them. I didn't see no sign of that.

Girl looked up at me, maybe eight years old, these big black eyes deep as Ed's used to be when he was thinking something out, long black hair down her back and a cute little pink skirt with pleats all around.

"What they call you?" I asked her and she answered bright as paint, "Isabelle but my name's really Tinkerbell."

"That what you want me to call you?"

"You going to be hanging around?"

"Depends on your grandma." Old lady'd gone off to the kitchen like she didn't want nothing more to do with me.

A pack of cards was laying on the table and I took it and spread the cards on the floor and showed those two how to shuffle and deal and we played Go Fish and they was laughing and Tinkerbell climbed on my lap and I knew it was going to work somehow.

The next night Grandpa looked at me with those big pale eyes and said, "I told you not to cut him loose."

"I didn't cut him loose, you did," I said, trying to keep my voice steady, but Grandpa just shook his head and walked away.

Well I had my work cut out for me and was glad of it. Went to Lily's trailer just about every morning early to get Tinkerbell and John out of the bed and feed them something, usually nothing much in the cupboards or the fridge so I commenced to bring eggs and bacon and such and fixed them a regular breakfast. Grandma didn't care for that, said I was messing up her kitchen, but I went right on and after a while she stopped bitching. Maybe she saw Tinkerbell was plumping up a little and had color in her cheeks, the boy not so much.

He wanted to tag after Grandpa Bear but the old man was getting cranky and said he couldn't abide no "unbroke kid" hanging around. So after a while that boy must have knowed there was nobody but me and he commenced to join in our games and walks and gained a little bit of weight—those two was so skinny!—and a little bit of color in his face and then one day he called me Auntie. So I went on all fall and winter with my two and woke up in the morning thinking first thing about seeing them and was glad.

Would you believe that went on for ten years?

Then their mom turned up with a new boyfriend and she was a drinker and so was he and by now my kids was teenagers and started to hang out with this man, name of Jerry. I couldn't do nothing about that or thought I couldn't but then Tinkerbell who'd growed up pretty as a picture and was seventeen and coming into bloom told me he put his hand up her skirt and pried between her legs and I went to the mama and told her the boyfriend had to go.

Well you can imagine she would not listen to me and I knowed I was going to have to get around her and somehow run that guy off.

Tinkerbell told me he whispered some fool message about meeting him that night in the old coal shed and I told her to do it. She started saying she never would but then I told her I'd be in a dark corner.

She played it big like something on television, put on her white lace nightgown and spread herself out on a blanket on the coal shed floor and I wanted to slap her face for the impudence but of course didn't.

After a while here he come, smelling to high heaven of the beer he'd been drinking all evening to drive up his courage. He went to kneeling by that girl and laying his hands on her and that's when I jumped out of that dark corner and landed right on his back. I'm pretty solid and he fell down on his face and I lay on him and bit his neck till the blood ran. Tinkerbell was laughing and he was screaming and cursing and run out of that shed like a dog with a can tied to its tail. Never did know what hit him in the dark. Oh he was a mess and knew it for that one minute if not never later or sooner. A mess, a stinking mess, and he didn't go near Tinkerbell after that.

We was tight as ticks from then on. John not so much, he was too much his Daddy,

saved up and bought himself this brokeback convertible with a top wouldn't close. Then he stepped right into Ed's shoes without even knowing it, in the bars most nights, rolling home after dawn and Grandpa Jake Bear too old and weak now to do nothing. I have to admit I wanted to see that bear skin rug again but that was not going to happen. I didn't have the arm strength to roll that boy up and Tinkerbell would have had a fit. She loved John the way I used to love Ed and John was headed the same way.

It was time for me to do something again so I got Tinkerbell to pack some stuff, saying we was going on a short holiday destination unknown and I put my things in a couple of cardboard boxes and we loaded up that brokeback convertible when John was still out cold and Tink slid his keys out of his pocket and shed some tears but went on with me.

We drove out of there, rising sun just wrinkling the eastern sky, and I thought if I never do anything else in my life I saved this girl.

We went on a seven-day tour of the close-in West, all them museums of stuff never had belonged to white people, pots, rugs, jewelry, but white people had bought or stole them some time back and put the pots and the jewelry in glass cases and hung the rugs on the walls and they did look swell.

"Them's all made by our people," I told Tink, "something to be proud about," but she was whining because I was not going to buy her a Navajo necklace with silver and turquoise beads and said, "If our people made it how come you can't get a special price?" But I knew better than go in that direction.

She went to whoring later but at least I thought she chose that way maybe and it was good money, more than Dairy Queen or Lottaburger, and I'll still be around when she's old and has to quit.

PRECIOUS

I was fixing to finally leave home when I turned twenty for a job in the Cities, electrical work I'd apprenticed for, but I had one more thing to do before I left the reservation. I told my cousin Tara what I was planning on and she got mad and said I had no business remembering but I didn't let her nor nobody else stop me because it was burning me and I had to find some way to get it out.

I had to remember the year I was six and Old Jake Bear, my grandpa, took me to the Jesuit boarding school.

Daddy Cowboy was drinking hard and even Mama Blacksleeves give up on the cooking and spent most nights at the casino losing a wad of money. So home was even less home and Tara and me was hungry.

I did what I could for Tara, got the snarls out of her long light-colored hair, and I expect it was seeing me at that work told Old Jake Bear I had to go. Combing a girl's hair is not boys' work nor men's neither.

He threw what few clothes I had in a garbage bag and was about to herd me down to his truck when he looked at my face. "Boy how long since you put a washrag to that mug of yours." He grabbed a rag and give my face a swipe. Then we was in the truck heading to town and I was scared to look back and maybe see Tara crying.

We pulled up to this big cement building where I knowed the Jesuits roosted like a flock of ravens. We all went up there Christmas for Mass and the free candy after. They was good men, those Jesuits, coming to pray for us sick or dying, never giving us money—we would have been shamed to ask—but giving us many warnings about our immortal souls. I used to wonder if our souls could be cut loose from our bodies that had so many problems—leukemia, high blood, a craving for sugar and beer and weed—set free to drift to the sky. I guess the good fathers would say that's what happens when we die but I wonder why we have to wait a whole life to get there.

When we got to the place Grandpa rung the big bell outside the front door and we waited a while before somebody come and opened. It was one of those we called "the browns" because they wasn't real monks yet and had to wear brown robes to show the difference. Smaller and younger too than the real ones and doing chores like sweeping and washing floors and answering the doorbell, not taking confession and leading the Mass.

Grandpa told this brown our business and he led us to their "parlor"—that's what they called their room for company—and told us to sit but since Grandpa was still standing, I stood too. Their parlor was dark with curtains over the window and big brown stuffed chairs I was scared to sit on and Mother Mary eyeing me from over the mantel.

After a while Father Joseph (I learned his name later) come in and Grandpa give him the garbage bag with my things and said, "Don't start that sniveling, boy," and turned and was gone. I didn't see him again till four months later at Christmas when we was all turned loose and he had to come take me home for a bit.

Us boys slept in this big long room, windows on one wall shivering in the wind and beds lined up on the other side. After supper and prayers and all that I washed in the tin basin a brown brought and got into that small little bed. I started to cry thinking how long I was going to be gone from home. I put my head under the pillow so the other boys wouldn't hear.

While my head was under the pillow I felt the mattress give and looked out and saw Father Joseph stretching himself alongside me.

A big long body.

He didn't have no robe on and when I rared up to

look at him, he smiled. "Don't you go making a commotion," he said, and I felt his big cold feet poking mine.

The only commotion I made was crying when he put his arms around me. I wanted that so bad and I knowed it was wrong.

I thought maybe that was the end of it, his arms around a lonesome boy homesick the first night in that place but he come the next night too and started to feeling up between my legs and I knew I ought to fight but his hand was warm and I was so cold. He made a mumbling sound like bees in a hive and then I felt something hard pressing in my thigh and I did say, "No, Father" and he pulled back and got up and left. But I knew that wasn't the end of it.

Now all these years later I had to remember I sort of wanted it—the warmth and the comfort and the pain that went along and that's what I have to spit out and get rid of.

"Help me, dear Father," I prayed that first night but I couldn't get no further 'cause "father" was a word I didn't know how to say no more.

He come most nights till I turned twelve. Daytime he never looked at me nor spoke to me. It was our secret he said, like the chocolate one of the boys smuggled in and hid under his mattress, eating it piece by piece all that long winter. "Precious," Father called what we did, a word I never had cause to use.

Father Joseph was my chocolate. How could I fight chocolate when I was starving?

Then I turned twelve and started growing hair where I never had hair. We had one bath a week and I was laying back in the warm water when Father Joseph knocked on the bathroom door like I had the right to say no.

Now I think I maybe I did have the right but I didn't know it then and he crept on in and sat on the edge of the bathtub and looked down at me naked in the water.

It was the way he was looking at me like a dog eyeing a bone that told me I had to stop it and I said, "No, Father" in my new almost man's voice and he looked at me like he was going to cry and then he got up and went away.

And that ended it after six years and I had nobody.

"Well you had me," Tara said when I told her, but she's just a girl and what does she know?

The spring I turned fourteen a big rumpus started about the boarding schools all over the country and what happened to the kids there that never come home. These guys started going around with their machines for poking down in the dirt, trying to find where all those kids was buried a long time ago aiming "to bring them home." Anybody with sense knows after so many years there's nothing left but who's gonna say such a thing? I saw them digging one day out back of the chapel where only the fathers was buried under their wooden crosses or that's what we thought. Toward the end of the day they come up with something and a big whoop went up.

It was the first graveyard where those guys actually found bones, kids' bones, and dug them up and took them to some laboratory to figure out what they was, I mean which tribe they come from.

The Jesuits was in a commotion and I heard one of the old ones say, "Where there's smoke there's fire, they'll be coming after us before you know it" and Father Joseph started looking at me with these sad dog eyes.

I heard what those eyes was saying but I acted like I didn't and thought the whole mess would blow over till one of the boys said he'd heard they was going to start asking everybody questions and I knew dog eyes was going to have to answer.

He caught me out back that evening emptying the dinner leftovers in the compost heap.

"Now, Sure Enough"—my nickname then—"you know that was nothing, just an old man trying the best he could to comfort a homesick boy."

There was a time I might have believed him or at least made like I did but that time was gone.

"No," I said and choked on that word "father" I swore I was not going to say no more.

"Well, my boy, you know you wanted it," he said, reaching out to grab my shoulder. "All those sly looks and shaking your little fanny."

"No!" I said. "And it don't make it right anyhow—you was father and I was just this lost kid."

"If they come here poking around and ask you—"

"I won't lie," I said.

"So you aim to ruin me!" he said, his breath hot and sour in my face. "Is that Christian? We're all sinners in the eyes of the Lord."

"That may be but I wasn't even growed."

And then my God he started to heave and cry, big tears coming down his cheeks. "What can I do? There's got to be something I can do to make it right," he said, pressing the crucifix hanging from his belt. "Christ came to earth to save sinners."

"Who's the sinner?" I asked him, by God getting the courage somewhere.

"You and me together," he said. "You and me together and that's what I'll tell them if they come for me."

Well, then I knew it would all get back to Grandpa Jake Bear and he'd beat me and maybe throw me out for good.

"All right," I told him. "I'm not going to say nothing."

He was so pleased he almost danced. "That's our promise to each other!" he started saying. "That's our promise to each other! It's precious!"

I guess he meant everything was OK. Not what I meant, but what could I do?

It wasn't much more than a week before they come, five of them, black suits, black hats, some kind of managers or lawyers or both together. I got called to the parlor where they was all sitting and one of them said, "Take a chair." The Head was there too. Then they waited for a while till the Head told me, "We called you here to ask you some questions about Father Joseph."

A tall dark man said, "There've been complaints, naming you. Be careful what you say."

I didn't wait for the question. "All that was a long time ago," I said.

"Did he touch you inappropriately?" the tall black asked.

"It was all so long ago."

"So long ago you might be remembering wrong?"

"I'm not remembering wrong," I said.

"Happened once and that was the end of it?"

"Went on for six years," I said, and a big flush of hot blood seeped up into my face.

"Did you tell him no?" another one asked me. "Did you tell him to stop?"

"Be careful, son," the first black said. "You're holding a good man's soul in the palm of your hand."

"You never did tell him no," the one who'd asked the first question said. "That's what he told us."

"I tried but he wouldn't hear me."

"You need to tell him now to his face," he said. "You

need to tell him you forgive him and ask him to forgive you too with the Lord's help."

"For what?" I said, and by God the tears started flying out of my eyes when I remembered Father Joseph telling me, "You wanted it too."

Then the door opened and Father Joseph come in.

"This young man here has something he needs to say to you," the Head said. "Kneel down, both of you."

I heard Father Joseph's knees creak and then he was down beside me.

I got up and shot out of there. I didn't look at Father Joseph but once. His face was slick like the surface of a paved road with rain on it. I thought maybe he'd been crying.

Then it was time for vacation and when I got home Tara was waiting for me and I told her part of it. She looked like she wasn't satisfied. "You didn't say nothing," she told me.

"I ruined a good man."

"Good!" she snorted, but over time when she saw Father Joseph was gone she did take some satisfaction. "You had a hand in it," she told me. "I'm proud of you."

She never did say that before or after.

I didn't see Father Joseph again. The kids told me he packed up and left that same day, sent to someplace in the Jemez Mountains where the priests in trouble go to get fixed.

After I heard that I told the whole thing to Tara. She didn't want to hear, told me it was wrong to fill her ears with that stuff but I went on anyhow and after I'd said it all we was both crying and I wasn't anywhere near ashamed.

She swore she wouldn't tell Grandpa and she kept her word so I went on living there as always.

I hardly ever think about it now. About the only part left in my mind is that word, "precious."

COWBOY AND THE WITCHES

I knowed what was going to happen after I clipped Tom Reynolds in the nose, him bothering me all the time was "my tribe" at Wounded Knee like I had to know or care. I felt something squish and then the blood streaming and him screaming and Mrs. Caruthers in charge of the play yard come flying. Turned out Tom's mother was on the school board and so it wasn't more than a day before Dr. Tucker called for a conference and Grandpa Jake Bear come to the school, Daddy being laid out after a five-day drunk celebrating the full moon.

Grandpa looked like a storm cloud sitting in the Head's office with Dr. Tucker stiff behind his desk, pictures of his pretty wife and children lined up in front of him like a fence.

"What you done now, boy?" Grandpa asked me like

I was always making trouble which I was not, at least not then.

I just looked at him.

"He seriously injured Tom Reynolds, broke his nose," Dr. Tucker said in that voice big enough to fill the world. "I can't allow violence in my school." It wasn't till later we found out about the school board mom.

"I want you to take him home today," he said to Grandpa in that tone didn't know how to deal with no. "Clean out your locker, boy, and get out of here." He stood up to let us know to go.

Grandpa didn't say nothing though I could hear him saying words in his mind. He grabbed me by the arm and pulled me. I took him to the lockers in the hall and cleaned mine out, not much in it just some books and papers I dropped in the garbage on our way out.

"You know what's going to happen," Grandpa said when we was both in his truck. He rammed his foot down, backed out of there so fast he made dust. "You going back up to the Jesuits if they'll take you."

We both knowed they'd take any boy believing as they do in sin but also in forgiveness, so I packed up the next morning didn't keep Grandpa waiting. I passed through our big room on my way out, saw Daddy laying on the floor, knew there wasn't no use saying goodbye.

We drove on up to the big house where the fathers roosted. I was nearly glad to be there 'cause I knowed them and they knowed me. Grandpa shoved me out of the truck, throwed my bag after me, peeled off in another cloud of dust.

A new young father I didn't know was waiting at the front door. "I'm Father Michael. Just call me Father Mike," he said which I had no plan on doing. "I looked up your record and put you back in that corner bed you liked."

I didn't think it made any difference but I seen he was trying hard so I thanked him and let him take my bag and followed him up those long wooden stairs. Seemed like my footprints from before was sunk in the wood.

At the top the dorm was just about the same except for what looked like new shades at the windows. Nobody there since it was class time and they was all in the other building doing they studies.

"I've got your schedule," Father Michael said and handed me a paper. He was close enough I could smell something sweet like aftershave but I don't believe the fathers used it. Deodorant as needed but no other kind of perfume. He had this young pink face seemed to call for special care.

He waited while I put what I had in the box under the bed, thinking how little that bed looked now I'd growed some but it would have to do. Then he took me to the class building saying I was a smart kid and knowed how to benefit from all they offered which was news to me.

The big room was full of boys and all them turned

to look when we come in the door and Old Man Greenstone that was reading them something said, "Come on in, Cowboy, we saved a special place for you" which wouldn't you know was in the dead center of the front row. "We're learning about the Romans this semester," he said, laying a fat book down on the desk arm of my chair. "You've got some catching up to do." They all went back to whatever they was doing before I come in—scratching, chewing a pencil, writing something Old Man Greenstone said.

Father Michael said, "Good luck to you, Cowboy, you've come to the right place" and went out.

Well it turned out they was reading about how the Romans in the old days murdered the Spartans at some mountain pass and all in all it was pretty fascinating.

At the end there was a big shuffle as we got up to leave and a few I remembered from before come to say hi and welcome back and so forth. Then it was time for lunch and the best grub I'd had in a while since Fat Annie flew the coop with that ranger. Daddy did the best he could but it never was much, hamburgers from Lottaboy on the highway about the best we could hope for and not many of them either. Some kind of soup full of carrots and potatoes with the sweet savor of beef in the broth and plenty of bread and second helpings allowed. Seems like they'd changed cooks or revolutionized Old Pete, the one they had.

I started to think I'd hit pay dirt. They give us a lot of reading but they wasn't anything we had to do after the last meal of the day at five p.m. so I got in the habit of carrying my books to the library and making a place at one of the big tables and before too long it was my place and nobody else ever sat there.

So it went on pretty good till November when Father Gordon called a special meeting and told us we was going to put on a play for the parents coming up to take us home for Thanksgiving. That was news to me, it hardly being likely Grandpa was going to drive all the way up here for a four-day vacation but never mind that—we was all going to do this play and Father Gordon was gung ho to get started and give out the roles.

Most of the boys was going to be soldiers that didn't have nothing to say and just was meant to stand around looking fierce. I thought that would be a fine choice for me but Father Gordon had picked out something different and if you asked me why I wouldn't have no answer.

"Cowboy, you're going to be one of the three witches," he told me. Willy who was kind of weak-minded and Saul, just a great big dummy, was going to be the other two.

It turned out the three of us was pretty near the start of the thing. Father Gordon handed out papers and started in on us practicing right away. He did tell the rest of them to leave which was a relief to me.

I was going to be Witch One and so it was up to

me to start. "When shall we three meet again"—that was some kind of foolish question since here we was meeting for the first time and hadn't done nothing yet. "In thunder, lightning, or in rain." Now, they was some good-sounding words and I appreciated them.

Witch Two was Willy who couldn't say the words right and it took Father Gordon a while to get him through "hurly-burly." That was a word not one of us had heard.

After Willy finally got it right it was the big dummy's turn 'cause he was Witch Three but he had it easy—just we was going to meet again before the sun set.

We went over and over those words, some of them not a one of us had ever heard before, like Graymalkin, some kind of witch cat, and Macbeth, which Father Gordon told us was the name of this thing.

One set of lines struck gold for me because I know "fair is foul and foul is fair" having seen it every day of my life.

That was it for the day and we went to dinner. Billy sat next to me and he started telling me he was going to be this lady called Macbeth and wear a crown. He was all worked up about it, said it made it almost OK they'd cut his hair the first day 'cause the crown would fit more comfortable. I never had growed my hair after my first time in that place and so no need to cut it.

Seemed like every one of the boys saw the fun in the thing and I didn't hear no grousing about going over some part with Father Gordon every day. They was a lot of fighting and talk of blood and murder most foul and I started to get the hang of it too.

Thirteen days later Father Gordon handed out what we was going to wear and it turned out us three witches got worn-out black robes the brothers didn't want no more.

Whoever had wore mine had a powerful stink and I come near to smothering first time I put it on but you can get used to anything if you put your mind to it so I didn't say nothing, knowing Father Gordon was doing the best he could. Next thing the three of us witches went to circling around a fake fire made out of crinkled up red paper with one of the kitchen big pots on top and that was some of the best words we had to say. Turned out Witch Two had been killing hogs and I was tormenting a sailor wife saying I was going to chase her husband gone to Aleppo though how I planned to do that sailing in a sieve nobody could tell. Witch Two said she'd give me a wind and Witch Three said she'd give me another and I told them they was kind. We had a whole lot of other things to say that didn't make any kind of sense but was pleasant on the ear.

Time passed quicker that month than usual. Billy went to parading around in his crown and swishing the big skirt of the fancy dress Father Gordon give him and Leo who was the king had a even bigger crown and a purple cloak and all the rest of us had things to do and words to say except for the crowd of soldiers. A few of them wanted to be put in the speaking parts but Father Gordon said his casting was done.

Then it come up to three days before Thanksgiving and a crowd drove in, every kind of car and truck you can imagine, old mud-streaked Plymouths and Dodges and even a Mercedes shined up like there weren't no tomorrow. Grandpa come rattling in his truck which I was not expecting.

I was in the library, run down the steps to see him. He was standing with the rest of the parents looking kind of lost and said to me right off, "I can't take you home it's a mess there right now." Turned out Daddy had asked some of his bar friends to come over for the weekend promising a big feed but no food in the house and so all of them drinking morning till night. Grandpa in his double-wide was going to steer clear and I was staying at school.

Father Gordon called for everybody in the play to go in back of the curtain he'd hung over the end of the refectory. Tables pushed to one side and rows of chairs set up. He had the clothes we was going to wear laid out in separate piles and we three witches got quick into our black robes 'cause we was going to be the first. The kettle was set over the crinkled red paper and we went to stand around it and Father Gordon jerked that curtain back and there they all was sitting and looking.

Willy got messed up on "hurly-burly" the way we knowed he would but finally spit it out with Father Gordon saying it for him from back behind somewhere. I didn't have no trouble with mine and Saul the fat dummy spoke up loud and clear and then we went off to wait at the side and the soldiers come in and stood around looking fierce. The king come in with some others and one of them was bleeding red paint down his arm and a soldier said he got cut saving the king from getting caught and the king was pleased and said he was a worthy gentleman, words new to me but pleasant.

Then the king and them went off leaving Jay who was some kind of smaller king and it was time for us three witches, and the first part was easy, just "hail hail hail," their way of saying hello.

I said right to Jay's face he was not as big as the real king which was true enough, him being only thirteen and not well growed but I told him someday he was going to be greater. Willy got out his line whole, saying Jay was not going to be happy like the real king but some way was going to be happier. Saul got to say he was going to beget kings and that drew a big laugh. Then we all said "hail hail hail" all over again and went off to one side and waited.

I looked out to see how Grandpa was taking it and he was right close in the second row and he weren't asleep.

A lot of what happened after that didn't make a

whole lot of sense to me but then Billy come wearing his crown and his queen dress and something about him was new. He commenced to read from a paper in his hand and the paper was shaking but his voice was smooth and thick and he had the fresh peach look of a girl and I couldn't hardly believe it because ordinarily he was scruffier than most. He talked on and on in that voice I'd never heard before, not a girl's but some kind of a mixture, and went to calling for the king so she could whip him with her tongue and by God I believed her. I caught on after a time that she and the king was going to murder Jay the little king while he was visiting them.

Turned out the Macbeth king didn't want to do it and Billy the queen had to work him, which she did saying "screw your courage to the sticking place" and now her voice was full of poison.

The Macbeth king got so scared he thought he seen a knife hanging in front of him and the queen had to come and work on him some more but he was still scared 'cause it seemed like he couldn't say Amen like he wanted. But even so he went away and when he come back his hands was red with paint blood and he was carrying two knives and the queen flew at him saying he was supposed to leave them at the murder scene so somebody else could be blamed.

He was the new king now but told the queen his mind was full of scorpions and heard some voice say he'd murdered sleep and that worried him and she had to shame him some to bring him up to the mark, saying how she'd tear off a baby sucking on her tit and dash its brains out if she had to before she'd cave in like him. She shouted that line out to everybody and I saw Grandpa get out of his chair like he couldn't take no more but then she quieted down and he sat.

It went on and on with three murderers and some kind of feast with big hunks of bread Father Gordon must have borrowed from the kitchen and then a ghost and I was getting awful hot in that black robe but then Father Gordon called the three of us to go round and round the pot again and I told the other two to throw some poisoned innards in and they did it as best they could having no innards just some muddy weed roots.

I had to put all kinds of horrid stuff in the pot, dragon scales and wolf's tooth and root of hemlock and even some piece of a Jew and that bothered me 'cause I knowed some of the parents was of that persuasion. Then we took the sticks Father Gordon had laid out and stirred that pot and called on what was in it to bubble bubble and Witch Two said if it got too hot he was going to cool it with baboon blood. By then I didn't even wonder where the baboon blood was going to come from.

That's when Grandpa Jake Bear stood up again and said he didn't plan on seeing any more of his grandson in a dress and was going to start his long drive home and a lot of the others got up and left too. Father Gordon pulled the curtain closed and it was done.

He was not pleased to shut the thing down before we had a chance to say the rest of the words like we was supposed to but I told him it had been a fine thing and not to let those folks who didn't know how to appreciate it take off the shine.

I never have forgot those words and say some of them now when I can't sleep like Eye of Newt and toe of frog though I don't know what Newt might be but I do know frogs. Father Gordon taught us some kind of strange magic bedded in a lot of words we didn't understand and someday I'm going to thank him.

It turned out I was the only boy staying at the school over Thanksgiving and even some of the fathers went off to see kin. They turned the heat down and the big rooms was so cold I stayed away from them and mostly stayed in the kitchen with Old Pete who kept the oven going, sat on a chair and put my feet up on the open door. Old Pete never did have much to say for himself and I didn't know where to start but it was companionable sitting there quiet.

Pete was punching down his dough to make a lot of loaves to freeze for when the boys come back and school started up again. I never had seen a man do that kind of work and I asked him if he minded but he told me it was better than the work he'd done before in Mexico which was digging ditches. He pulled off a pinch of raw dough and handed it to me and it tasted good.

It got old sitting there all day so I started to wander around and ended up in the chapel. That was the prettiest room in the place because of the big colored window over the altar. All times of day the colors shone bright enough to give you a headache, the red and the blue in particular and the gold bright enough to melt. I sat in a pew off to one side so as not to be blinded and from there the blue of the Jesus' robe shone but softly. He was wearing his halo and had a sick-looking lamb under his left arm and he was barefooted.

I knowed from all the Bible readings he was poor but he was also a king and so why no shoes. Nobody to ask so I made up a story, how he'd had shoes, good leather ones, but saw a beggar bare foot in the street and took the shoes off and give them to him, even stooped down and put them on the beggar's stinking feet.

That would never happen in this day and age but maybe way back then.

I'd been kind of downhearted being the only kid not home for Thanksgiving and Pete saw it and said he was going to cook me something special for that day and asked me didn't I have anything to be thankful for. It took me a while to dig it up but sitting there looking at the barefoot king with his sick lamb I knowed we was heading into the darkest coldest time of the year but called to mind how late February there's always a four-day thaw and the owls start to hoot calling each other to mate and the little white flowers they call snowdrops Fat Annie dug into the yard before she run off with the ranger would be coming up. Little white bells on the bare dirt. So there was two things and I told Pete and he said they was good.

Then I thought of something else and told him Eye of Newt and he liked the sound of it just as much as I did and asked me to say it again instead of a blessing when we sat down to eat our Thanksgiving chicken.

BELTS

This morning while I was waiting on the blacksmith I started to recall what my grandpa Old Jake Bear used to do with his belt when I was still a kid they called Sure Enough. No telling how or why or when these memories come up from the bottom of my mind. Horseshoes and belts and my mare holding her hoof up—some link I can't see.

I used to see his belt curled on the kitchen counter or stretched along the edge of his bed or waiting on the arm of his chair and we knew, my cousin Tara and me, Old Bear knew how to use it.

Daddy Cowboy was different. Wore a belt but never took it out of his pants. That changed after Father Michael from the mission started coming by. The priest taught him not to put up with our shenanigans, which was never much, just cutting school and stealing a bottle of beer. So once or twice Daddy pulled out his belt but his heart wasn't in it and Tara and I just got out of the way.

I liked the old priest. He was one of the good ones, don't let nobody tell you there wasn't any. I thought he was a thousand years old but found out later he was forty-two at the time I'm recalling. He was black head to toe as they was in those days but one time when the creek flooded the road and he had to cross to get to us, I seen him hike up them black robes and he had hairy legs and after that I thought of him more as something regular.

Nobody else ever had the time or the wish to visit us. The men—Old Bear, Daddy, Uncle Joe, and whatever hired hands we had around—was always going off to mend fence or feed horses, and the women, whoever happened to be in the house married into us or just hanging around hoping, had the cooking and cleaning and grousing to do so sitting around shooting the breeze was just a waste of time. Whereas Father Michael would sit with us half the day reading his missal.

The summer I turned eighteen Pat come back on leave from Iran, bigger than I'd ever expected to see, my oldest brother but kind of a weeny before he enlisted. Now every inch of his uniform was filled out and his shoulders looked ready to punch out of his jacket and his belt was more than something to hold up his uniform pants. Tara who always had a crush on Pat (he never noticed) asked me, "You think he could whip that belt out fast?" and I told her I expected he could if there was a reason. But there never was no reason.

He got to scratching on me about going back to community college (I dropped out after my first semester, wasn't nothing there I wanted to learn), saying I could get sprung from the rez with an education.

"I don't much want to get sprung," I told him. Tara was shooting me one of her looks, meaning go easy.

"You can't sit around here on your butt the rest of your life," Pat told me and I almost went "Can too" like I was seven years old but didn't.

"Government subsidies keep us fed regular," I said, "and I like being with family." I said that even though most everybody was gone. Tara and me and some drop-in cousins coming for a meal was all that was left.

"Get out and see the big world," Pat said. His leave was up and he was fixing to go. We waved him off the porch and went back to whatever we was doing at the time.

We have this house, Tara and me. Not much but ours. Big room, bathroom, kitchen. Anybody can see it's our house now everybody is dead or gone. Tara hung her Jesus on velvet in the big room where the colors catch the first light of morning and my fishing poles are stacked by the door. Not much fishing these days since the copper mine dumped poison in the creek but that'll clear up in time. We still got five horses and the mama goat Tara wanted chomping weeds by the porch and fences galore to keep track of.

Every now and then Tara declares a holiday and we sit on the porch and look out over our land, mostly gone to thistle and walking stick cactus but all ours. Where would we find that in "the big world"? We couldn't afford to buy a quarter acre and here we own twelve hundred and twenty, all the way to the foot of the Bitter Root Mountains. That's land we inherited from Daddy and Old Bear, land the Feds owed us after they took everything else a long time ago.

We act like we own it but we don't really. Father Michael told us that. "Your great-grandfather left it to your grandfather and he left it to your father but he didn't make a will so the court will have to decide."

It meets down in Helena, no idea what goes on here.

"I'm Daddy's only son now Pat's gone," I said, "killed by a sniper last day of his second tour."

"God rest his soul," Father Michael said like it was no surprise to him. "In the midst of life we are in death. I don't know what the law says about land left intestate." He was rocking back on his stool. He never accepts a chair, says sitting on a stool makes him keep his back straight. "We'll just have to see."

The court didn't get around to considering it, they mostly leave us alone and so Tara and I plan on staying here the rest of our lives unless something better turns up. Which don't seem likely.

That same year I turned eighteen Grandpa Jake Bear got sick and died and was put up on the scaffold—tribe singers always put up there so the birds eating them learn their songs. He was the last of us to be done that way now the singers are gone and there's an undertaker in Sheridan and everybody wants a burial proper. His belt got put in a garbage bag with everything else which wasn't much.

Time passed as it always does and then late one winter when I was twenty-five Father Michael come by and told me he was going to visit the old folks up at the far end of the rez and I jumped right in and asked him to take me with him. The old folks go there when they don't want to be bothered no more, just waiting to die.

"You never visit so you don't know what's going on," Father Michael said.

"I was there a long time ago. I don't remember much. Now I just leave them be."

"Then you probably never learned the rules. You don't just barge in on one of the old folks' houses. You wait outside the door till somebody invites you in."

"I can do that," I told him.

"And then you stay quiet till one of them asks you something."

"I can do that too. I'm wondering why you pick this time to go. Hind end of winter, mud and ice everywhere."

"I want to see where your grandfather is. Nobody else to do it, seems like."

"He's been gone seven years, scaffold might have fallen down by now. What time do we leave?"

"Eight a.m. Monday and spend the day."

It was Friday, giving me the weekend to cogitate, not that it ever occurred to me not to go. Old Jake Bear deserved some attention it seemed to me.

I was up in good time and when Father Michael's headlights come through the front window I hopped out the door and run to the car. It was going to be a first for me, time with Father Michael to add to the usual dibs and dabs. As I said I liked him.

He's a priest and a good one but his driving is something else. He can't keep off the center line and he has one of them new cars that lets you know it. That buzzer went off every minute and I finally asked him could he turn it off but he said he didn't care to and besides didn't know how. So that thing kept going off. It sure interrupted the flow.

Still he got in some words: Did I know where my mother was? I said I didn't. I wasn't going to tell him she run off a long time back and nobody ever wanted to talk about her. Turned out Father Michael already knew.

"You know why she left?" Father Michael asked me.

"I asked Daddy but he said to keep my nose out."

"He beat her up," Father Michael said, all business.

"One too many times and she was sick of it and lit out."

"Maybe he had a reason," I said, not wanting the old priest to get a bad opinion of Daddy.

"There never is a reason," he told me sharp, "though men white brown or any color always claim there is."

I'd never known him to come down so hard on the side of righteousness. Most of the time Father Michael was pretty easy on us, never give it to us for getting drunk or running off with some dumb girl. I expected it was going up to see the old folks that made him mean. Likely he was scared. I know I was.

Of course it's my people, my dad's and grandpa's and going way further back but over time we kind of lost touch.

It was most noon when we got to the first old-style house and I tell you that place kind of amazed me. Remember I was a kid when I saw it too little to know what to think. Now I saw the trash piled up on the side of the house and the old flea-bitten hound sleeping in the road and the kids playing in the mud.

Nobody grown was in sight but Father Michael knew where he was going and stopped in front of the second of the old-style houses, a sort of cabin made out of unpeeled logs. That meant to me old people, maybe even somebody who'd known Jake Bear. There was space for a little garden out front and a swing on the porch just like someplace respectable.

I followed Father Michael up on the porch. He tapped on the door. Then he sat down on a bench and motioned me to sit by him. I guess we waited ten or fifteen minutes looking out at the road and I knew somebody was studying us through the window. After a while the door opened and Father Michael took that as an invitation and I followed him in.

It was dark in there, smelled of sage. I thought the place was empty, then I saw two eyes bright as hawk's shining at me through the dark and Father Michael said, "Say hello to your grandma, boy," though how he knew I couldn't tell you.

A claw come out of the darkness and grabbed me and reeled me in and I was stuck up against this flat chest that smelled like VapoRub.

"Great-grandson," she was saying, "I thought to die without never seeing you," and I knew then another reason why Father Michael wanted to visit. He always said families should stick together "for the glory of God" but with the amount of trouble we get into I don't think we've got much time left over to glorify.

The old folks believe in sticking together too. Lots of them went to the Jesuit boarding school where Father Michael teaches and some still go to the mission church, but when AIM got big they'd use any excuse to talk bad about the priests. Lots of phone calls to Daddy ranting and raving. And there was some bad ones I know but one rotten apple don't really spoil the whole barrel.

Grandma had something stewing in a old black iron pot and I suspicioned it had been there for some while and maybe growing mold but I was too hungry to say no, besides it's being rude, so when she handed me a bowl I took a good sniff—no mold, plenty of chile—and dove right in. So did Father Michael, and Grandma watched us eat like it was doing her heart good. Seems like those old-time women live to feed anybody comes through the door. That's why she kept that big black pot going on the stove.

After we'd eaten all we could hold—Grandma didn't take a bite, that was always the way with those women, they lived on air—Father Michael wiped his mouth on his sleeve and said, "We came to see you but also to check on Old Jake Bear."

She pursed her mouth. "He's up the hill."

"Been seven years since he went. Anybody go up there to check?"

"Well I can't walk that far with my bad knee and it may be nobody else thinks about it."

"That's what I figured. So with your permission this young man and I are going up there now."

"Well," she said, "I can't tell you no."

So we went out the back door and started up. Not a big hill but steep and we was both puffing by the time we got to the top.

The view seemed like it stretched all the way to the

plains and even on that dark winter day I thought it was grand and remembered some old-timer telling me that's why they planted the rez there a long time ago. Like the old folks was counting on climbing that hill and looking at the view every day and for all I know that's what they did in the olden times though I suspect it was more the good hunting and the river not too far away.

There right in front of us was the scaffold: saplings and some bigger trees six feet tall, fastened together with nets of vines. The vines was dried out and some of them cracked and broken so the wood platform at the top was slanted. Old Jake Bear in his wrapping had skidded to the edge and looked about to fall.

"We've got our work cut out for us, boy," Father Michael said.

"They wouldn't want us to touch him," I told him.

"Just let him fall down?"

"Whatever. We don't have the right."

"Well I'll sanctify us," he said, and dug out his missal.

"That's not their kind of sanctifying," I said but he kneeled down and went on like he never heard me.

He started to read in his church voice, "O God whose mercies cannot be numbered, accept our prayers on behalf of thy servant Jake Bear and grant him an entrance into the land of light and joy in the company of thy saints." He looked up. "That's in case he's still stuck in purgatory" which seemed more than likely the way he'd lived. Then Father Michael got up and made the sign of the cross at the scaffold five or six times.

I said, "He never had much truck with saints."

"He does now," Father Michael said. "Let's get to work."

We went and stood under the scaffold and looked up and I saw it was going to be a job.

"Get out your knife and go cut some fresh vines," the old priest told me.

So I went in the brush and found a bunch of creeper and cut twelve long vines and brought them back. Father Michael started to peel off the old vines and that made the platform tilt more and Old Jake slid off and hit the ground in a cloud of dust.

"Now you've done it," I said. Father Michael was crouched down looking at Old Jake in his wrappings that was torn in four places where the ravens had got in.

"Now we have to get him back up," he said, standing up.

"We can't touch him," I said, "it's not right."

"Is it right to leave him laying on the ground for the coyotes?"

I didn't have nothing to say to that. It's usually birds do that work.

He made the sign of the cross on Old Jake and then he told me to start lacing the new vines in place of the old.

I got the vines up pretty good and then we pushed the platform straight. Old Jake had to go up next. "All right," Father Michael said. "Climb on my shoulders."

I never had touched this man let alone climbed on him. "No," I said but he crouched down and waited and I knew he'd stay that way till I climbed on. I put one foot on his shoulder and then the other one on the other shoulder and when he started to straighten up I nearly lost my balance and had to grab a hold of his hair. I knew I was pulling but the groans coming out of him was because of my weight and not what I was doing to his hair. It was smooth and shiny and almost white and I had two full handfuls as he come up straight and I thought, This is a priest who's never been touched by man or woman and here I am riding his shoulders and grabbing his hair.

Once he straightened up I crawled on the platform and looked out over the valley and saw the river shining way off. It seemed like the top of the world. The wind smelled like pinion and fresh water.

"Can you raise him?" I asked.

He squatted and reached for Old Jake's shoulders inside his wrapping and dragged him upright and heaved him higher till I could reach him leaning down and grabbing and hoping the wrapping didn't come apart. It held good and I scooted him onto the platform and flattened him out. He weighed next to nothing after all that time, but he humped up till I flattened him.

Then I slid down. For that one minute Father Michael and I stood face to face. But then he went too far telling me to read off the whole burial service from his missal.

"He got prayed over when they put him up. I'm not going to add words he never heard," I said and I must have sounded pretty fixed because Father started reading the service himself and the wind swept his words away so Old Jake couldn't have been mortified.

When he was finished we went down the hill and straight out to his car and I knew Grandma was watching us through the window. I was glad we didn't stop by. Nothing we could say would make what we did right by her.

In the car I started to feel the hot of anger that's gotten me into trouble so many times but still I had to let it out in words. "You white people took just about all we had a long time ago. Can't you even leave us our dead?"

"Don't want that old man disrespected, torn up by whatever animal comes by, bones dragged down to the village."

"Well we fixed that but how come you had to say all those words?"

"For everlasting life, boy, don't you want that for him?"

"Up there with the angels in the white nightgowns?"

Father Michael did something then I never knew him to do before or since. He reached out and give me a smack across the mouth. It wasn't much of a smack but when he lifted his arm to do it his cassock rode up and I seen he was wearing a belt, black like the one I used to see on the bathroom sink.

We rode back with that warning beep coming on every minute when Father Michael crossed the line. He let me out at my front door and leaned across the seat and asked me to forgive his brothers for everything they'd done.

Now, those are words I'd never heard before and I think there maybe were tears in his eyes so what did I do but start bawling and run up the steps to get away from him.

Because forgive one old priest maybe I will do but I'll never forgive all the rest of them and what they done though I know Father Michael was one of the good ones and don't let anybody tell you different.

Yes he was wearing a belt but it was just to hold up his pants.

ASHES

First thing that morning Father Jerome told the boys at Saint Paul's the Jesuit boarding school they was going to get ashes. Cowboy planned to skip that—March cold and bleak enough there on the Northern Plains without adding some kind of penalty, made no sense to him at all—but then Father Jerome caught him between the refectory and the classroom.

"You told me yourself your dad beat you for no reason," Father said, face so white in his black robe he looked like a ghost.

"Well he did once or twice but his heart wasn't in it," Cowboy muttered.

"Speak up, boy, I can't hear you."

The other boys crowding past was looking to see what kind of terrible trouble Cowboy'd gotten into because from his first day back when he'd climbed a tree to get up on the roof they'd pegged him for a badass. Cowboy didn't mind. Better that than one of the whiners wet the bed at night and cried for what seemed like hours keeping the other boys awake.

"I said I probably did something."

"But you didn't know what you did then and you don't know now and I see in your eyes you're harboring un-Christian thoughts against your dad."

Cowboy looked off but Father put out his hand and pushed his chin around. "That's why I want you to get your ashes, to show you're a sinner. You ever have them?"

"No," Cowboy said though the truth was his cousin Tara did take him one time to the church in town told him he had to kneel down and let the priest daub the ashes on his forehead but that was a long time before so Cowboy didn't think to tell it.

"I want to see you on your knees at the altar," Father said, taking his skinny cold hand away. "You've got a lot to confess."

It was going to happen right away which meant missing breakfast. Cowboy tried to fill up the hole in his stomach thinking about extra pancakes—Julio in the kitchen always saved some for him, cold by then but filling. Thinking about the pancakes didn't help much and when three of the fathers come and started to herd the boys into the chapel Cowboy knew he was going to have to do something.

The big fat father was standing outside the door to the kitchen and Cowboy knew he was fat but also strong and could catch a boy by the ear or the hair and hold on till hell froze over.

He pushed his way with both elbows out through the boys into the kitchen. Julio was sitting on his stool. Cowboy smoked with him sometimes outside the back door. When he saw Cowboy acting the runaway Julio pointed to the back door and Cowboy was there in a hop, skip, and jump and shot out into the clean cold air.

He ran up to the top of the hill where he went sometimes to look out at the plains spreading away further than he could see and placed the ranch and Daddy and the rest of them somewhere at the edge of his seeing and knew they was there, they was always there, and he would get back to them or they would come get him one of these days.

From the hill he looked down on the steeple and saw a river of boys going through the big doors, fathers herding them along the way you herd sheep. Nobody looked up and saw Cowboy watching.

The chapel bell commenced to clang and Cowboy knew Sebastian who brown-nosed Father Jacob was inside the chapel pulling on the rope, supposed to be a favor though Cowboy didn't know why. On special days when there was four services, sunrise, noon, evening, and midnight, Sebastian had raw red hands from pulling the rope.

Cowboy knew he wasn't safe on the hill, sooner or later one of the fathers would come looking for him. It was his special alone place and they knew that and would look there first.

He ran down the other side of the hill and crossed the field to the barn. The four horses was there and more likely than not one of the hired hands feeding them or mucking out stalls but maybe because it was ashes day nobody was there when Cowboy pushed open the big wooden doors.

Right away he heard the horses munching and guessed they'd had their oats early, and went in the first stall—that was Star the chestnut gelding—and he looked up from his trough, saw it was Cowboy he knew well, and went back to munching. Cowboy had gotten him out of the stall a few times and galloped him bareback across the field till the fat father come running, big belly jolting, and caught Star by his mane. Detention for Cowboy for a week but it was worth it to feel Star galloping under him and the wind in his hair.

Cowboy leaned his head against Star and heard his throat moving when he swallowed and smelled the sweet strong smell of a well-tended horse that knew his work, pulling the wagon to the field and back, and was brushed every night. There was no dander in his hair and it felt smooth against Cowboy's cheek.

Star was not a riding horse. All the horses in the

barn were workhorses—nobody had time to ride them and what would be the point anyway? When one of the fathers went to town for supplies he took the Ford truck.

Cowboy went in the tack room and found a good piece of rope hanging on a nail and brought it back to Star's stall and looped it over his neck. By then the gelding was through eating and turned his head and looked at the boy.

"We're getting out of here," Cowboy said, and jumped off the ground onto Star's back.

The feel of the gelding's spine under him was the feel of being a child and he clamped his knees to the gelding's sides and got him out of the stall and through the big doors.

There in front of him was the field they cropped for corn but now at the end of winter there was nothing left but a few stalks leaning to the dirt and some patches of snow and ice.

The wind was rustling Cowboy's hair and he wished he'd thought of his hat but what difference did it make. The wind was cold but in February that was what always happened and he knew how to stiffen himself against it and that kept him almost warm. He set his heels into Star's sides and the gelding broke into a trot and then with some more push a canter and then with a sharp dig a gallop and they was flying though the field, clearing the downed cornstalks and the patches of snow and ice, Star moving like he'd waited a long time for another chance to be free.

At the far side of the field there was a old barb wire fence and Cowboy thought to head for the gate but Star had his own opinion of the matter and left the ground with a big push and a groan and jumped the barb wire, coming down so hard on the other side he came close to unseating Cowboy.

But that never had happened in all the years of his growing up and if it had he'd have been given a good swat because "We don't fall off horses in this family" and though the swat hurt, Cowboy would've known it was only good and right.

They was galloping down the dirt road he knew led in eight miles to town and Cowboy was wondering whether those swats that did happen although not because of him falling was what Father thought Cowboy had to forgive. He didn't see the need since they was all in the day's work.

A big old farm truck come huffing down the road and passed in a cloud of dust but Star stayed steady under Cowboy's hand like he knew they was heading to town and needed to keep up a good pace.

Cowboy knew the drill when one of the boys ran away because somebody ran just about every week. The tribal cops would be out in their vehicles in no time with three or four of the fathers jammed in the Ford truck coming on behind. No boy was ever gone for more than a couple of hours.

The eight miles of the dirt road went by with nobody in sight and Star drew up panting in front of the drugstore that had an old-timey fake front on it like most of the little stores in that place because of a movie made there years before.

Cowboy carried no money and had no need of buying anything though a Dr. Pepper would have come in handy. He rode Star at a slow pace to the park in the middle of town. Nobody was there. Then he saw a small table with a white cover on it and a little priest standing behind it.

He rode closer and saw it was a lady priest. She was not much bigger than a child and her black robe was long on her and the white collar looked loose around her skinny neck. She was standing there behind her little table with a lighted candle on it and she had a silver-looking box in her hand.

"Ashes?" she said to Cowboy when he rode up.

"Maybe for my horse," he said, thinking he was smart.

She walked right up to Star and dipped her pointer in the silver box and made two crossed marks on Star's forehead and the gelding stood quiet as though prepared.

Then she said, "Bow down before the Lord" and Cowboy half expected Star to get down on his knees but he went on standing so Cowboy slid down and did what the lady priest told him and stayed on his knees in the dirt.

The lady priest went on in that drone they all had, "Grant, most merciful Lord, to your faithful..." She stopped there and then went on, "creatures pardon and peace that they may be cleansed from all their sins."

"Star never done nothing," Cowboy said, "except maybe giving that mare Jenny a little nip when she got to the hay ahead of him and she had that coming."

"Greed is one of the seven deadly sins," the little priest said, not in the drone but in her ordinary white lady voice. "What about you, young man?"

"I'm not greedy, I'm starved," Cowboy said. "I had to get out before breakfast."

She put her hand on his head and he felt it was warm.

"Why'd you do that?"

"The fathers was pushing us all in the chapel to get the ashes."

"Are you afraid of ashes?" she said, her voice soft as a feather.

Cowboy looked up and saw her little peaked nose like some kind of tiny bird beak. "I'm not afraid of ashes," he told her, "but Father told me I had to confess first."

"Why didn't you want to?" she asked and Cowboy knew from her ordinary voice they had run out of whatever she'd learned to say.

"I don't know what to confess," he said and had to

duck his head to hide his shame. There was no way he was going to tell her he touched himself at night for the relief of it or any of the rest of it.

"We are all sinners in the eyes of the Lord," she said and now she had the drone again.

"Well then I don't see the use. Star didn't sin but you put the ashes on him. What's that supposed to mean?"

"So he knows the Lord forgives him if he nips that mare again."

"Then I guess he's got to forgive me. I never did nothing worse than that." It was a lie and he knew it and felt it burn like a fire-heated brand.

"Of course he forgives you," she said and her hand was still warm on his head. "He always forgives you. Now I'm going to place your ashes."

He stiffened himself, thinking it was going to burn worse than the brand but then he felt her finger just above his nose and it was light as cottonwood fluff. "Remember you are dust and to dust you shall return," she said in a voice that was not drone and was not ordinary.

Cowboy started to get up but she pressed him down. "Have mercy on me, oh Lord," she started and now her voice was halfway to a shout and Cowboy felt other people coming near. "In your compassion blot out my offenses." He knew she said it for him whether he wanted her to or not.

Cowboy felt somebody big kneel down next to him

in the dirt and the little priest stepped over with her silver box and started the whole thing again.

He stood up. Five people was waiting and he stayed to see the first one get up with the dark gray cross on his forehead and the next one kneel down and then he turned and led Star off. If he'd had any change on him he'd have put a little something on the white table to pay for Star's blessing.

Not for his.

The little lady priest with her pointy nose was too nice to know all he'd really done, stealing Granddaddy Jake Bear's cigarettes regular by the time he was ten, sipping out of his Daddy's whisky bottle to celebrate turning eleven and sure to go on from there, kicking his aunt Bonnie Blue in the pussy and laughing when she cried, tying a tin can to the tail of the old dog they called Prince and chasing him out of the yard and trying to put his thing in the bitch that belonged to Uncle Joe and would have done it too if she hadn't of run off. And all that was just the start of it. So how was God going to forgive him when he didn't even know what all Cowboy had already done?

He knew he'd do worse later.

He thought the tribal cops would be coming for him soon with a bunch of fathers close behind and he didn't care what they did to him when they caught him but he didn't plan to wait to hear the cop car siren going, that terrible scream that started the hairs up on the back of his neck. He jumped on Star and started back to the school at a good pace and got there before anybody noticed he was gone because they was all busy in the chapel with the ashes.

A long time later when he and some of the other boys that was all men now lit that chapel on fire and burned it to the ground he thought of the little lady priest in her long black robe that was too big for her and her white collar loose around her skinny neck and knew she would still put the cross on him if she had the chance and felt it burn in his flesh worse than any brand.

COWBOY AND THE FOOT

"Why'd you do it, Grandpa?" Little Squirt Georgie asked me, son of that Mexican lady no fault of hers dad never did nothing for her or his boy. Ended up back here when Georgie weren't nothing more than a squaller. He now gets dropped off with me whenever his mom makes it known she has to go down south to the "spa" for the sake of her mental health.

I took a liking to the little bugger, White Lady used to say he was the apple of my eye. I don't know nothing about that but the truth is—I've had it happen before—if I change them stinky diapers and get up in the night with a bottle to stop the screaming I take a liking to whichever one is causing the commotion. Don't want to admit to it or the squaller be left with me permanent.

Now "Why'd you do it, Grandpa?" I don't normally answer questions figuring whoever is plaguing me can find out some other way but this being Little Squirt Georgie I give it a try.

"Wasn't my fight, I knowed that all along, but Jose been a good friend of mine said he needed help. Met him two a.m. on the county road, got in his truck rode to where that thing was standing. City should have more sense than plant it right where county road and main road meet. Thousands pass it every day and somebody bound to get riled."

"What'd it look like?"

I get up to freshen my coffee. Pot empty with that burnt smell. I wash it out and put the old grounds back in (they good for three cups), fill it with water set it on the stove. I look back at Georgie waiting for me on the stool, wouldn't move from that spot without my story. Little white-haired seven-year-old with eyes sky blue no sign of dark skin—maybe just as well.

"What'd it look like, Grandpa?"

"Just one of them Spanish. Juan Onate come up here long time ago wanting to give the whole place to Spain or was it Mexico...just about the same if you ask me."

"Yeah but what did it look like?" He was a plaguer.

"Big. Maybe seven, eight foot tall. Armor everywhere. Great big helmet on top, you couldn't make out the face. Gold all over. I thought it was real gold but turned out not to be. City was saving money."

"How'd you and Jose cut it?"

"Well it weren't steel or we'd have been out of luck. Jose took his hacksaw to it, made a cut at the ankle above the boot. Sliced right in. Thing made out of some kind of composite, I don't know exactly what, but Jose's saw bit right in. Made a big hole. I went to pulling on the right boot and it wouldn't come off. Jose cut through on the other side I took a good hold and pulled the boot off. Whatever was inside it stood for the foot come clear too."

"What'd you do with it?"

"Jose took it. I don't know, probably hauled it to the dump with his trash."

"I still don't see the reason you cut that foot off," Little Squirt said.

"Jose's from Acoma. Those folks still nursing a grudge over what that Onate did way back. They fended him and his army off for quite a while, sitting up on top of their mesa throwing rocks down. Only two ways up and one barricaded. Would have held them off forever but somebody showed Onate the other way up. Come up behind the warriors, caught and tied them, sawed off the men's right feet."

"That's terrible! Didn't they bleed to death?"

"Probably. Winners get to do what they want, you'll learn that one of these days unless you always win which don't seem likely. Jose was carrying the grudge for his people, reason he asked me to help him saw off that foot."

"But Grandpa that's against the law."

"Against the law too for them to jail me for killing that white officer when all I done was watch. Jose the only friend who come all that way to visit me in the pen. I owe him something."

Little Squirt seemed like he was satisfied, went in the kitchen to see what he could grab, come back turned on the TV.

We was halfway through some show he fancies when the lights started to play across the wall. I was expecting it.

"Go open the door," I told Georgie.

"I want to see—"

"Never mind that, go open the door." I wanted them officers to see they's a child in the house.

He went. Door opened, Big Fred and his partner they call Little Fred—that's not his name—come in all braced up carrying all kinds of heat. Police these days like a walking armory: nightstick, cuffs, poison spray, big black pistols already halfway out of the holsters. Asked my name like they didn't already know it—they got rules—shoved some papers at me. "Accessory to a crime."

"Well at least you got that right," I say, standing up slow so my knees don't creak.

Little Squirt starts to scream.

"They just taking me to the courthouse," I tell him.

He grabs my hand little fingers like pincers. "I'm going with you!"

"Where's his mom?" Big Fred asks me.

"Gone down to the spa, won't be back till dark."

"Well somebody's got to take him—" Little Squirt's hanging on and screaming.

"Hand me that phone."

Little Fred obliges.

Most the time I don't have reception but wouldn't you know this time I do. Called up Great-Auntie Tara—she's retired.

"Police here to get me," I tell her. "Come on over here, take George."

She must of heard him screaming. "Well I got to dress," she says.

I tell the Freds, "She's on her way. Sit down. You want coffee?"

They have to say no, that's rules too but they do sit down.

"Now George, stop that screaming. Nothing bad's going to happen to me."

He burrows in my lap. Boy don't have much in this world. Dad gone so long he don't know he has one mom always trying to get away somewhere.

George stands up, straightens himself, turns to the

Freds, starts telling them the Acoma story. "That's why Grandpa had to do it. And it was Jose made the cuts."

"Your grandpa's a accessory, that's all, son," Big Fred says.

George don't know that word but it pacifies him.

Big Fred and I was at school the same years so I start him telling about the trouble we got into—Little Fred tries to stop him don't get nowhere. Time passes till Tara come huffing and puffing in the door. Pretty town dress, full makeup and all.

"What you gotten into now?" all that. George don't want to go to her so I give him a firm push.

Big Fred is aiming to cuff me, then has the consideration not to do it in front of the boy. "Lets' go."

"I got to weewee," I tell them, "'less you want me to wet them nice leather seats in your patrol car."

"Go on but make it quick," Big Fred tells me.

"Don't worry, I got experience," I say, going in the bathroom, close the door lock it. They commence to knocking right away. I climb up on the commode, push the window open, jack myself out on the ledge, drop down and run. By the time they come around the corner I'm gone gone gone.

Well more or less just down in the weeds on other side of the barn. They's running every which way shouting cursing, after a time give up and drive off. I heard Big Fred say, "We'll get the SOB later today. He always goes to the Big Z around sunset to start his drinking." I think, Boy, you way out of date. White Lady got me started at AA a year ago last winter and I ain't hardly been in a bar since 'cept once in a while for company.

Well now what, I think. I'm too old to spend a night out with it still hitting freezing before dawn, that old wrecked barn not much of a shelter. I start off walking to Great-Aunt Tara's, get there and knock on the door. She come out looking like a tornado, little Georgie hanging on to her hem, letting loose when he sees me and run to me, grabs me tight.

"Well here you come like the bad penny," Great-Auntie say. The little squirt is hollering, "Grandpa Grandpa they turned you loose." She starting to soften up a little, I seen it in her face.

"Listen, all I done was go along with Jose when he cut off that foot."

She come pretty close to smiling reminding me what she looked like when she was young. "We all hated that thing, city should've had more sense than put it where we have to drive by every damn day. You not one of them crazy Acomas, so how come you had to go along?"

I'm still standing outside. "Let me in I'll tell you the whole."

"Well for about five minutes, I got laundry in the machine."

I go in. "Jose drove all that way visited me in the

pen when none of the rest of you couldn't figure out how to do it."

"Jose don't have responsibilities."

"Well whatever, I still owe him. All I done was drive over with him stand and watch."

Little Squirt has to pipe up. "Grandpa, you said you pulled off that foot!"

"Well wouldn't you know!"

Tara come close to laughing. "So now you can't go back to your place."

"They'll have it staked out."

She says, "I got to go to town tomorrow, you come on in stay take care of this boy while I'm gone."

"Yes ma'am," I say.

Little Squirt is dancing a jig.

"Hope you'll let me bunk here tonight," I say.

"Might as well. Go on over to the store and get something for dinner."

I take her truck. Squirt rides with me going on all the way about "them policemens." Scared him but he also admires, big guns and so on. We pick up some steaks I don't scant on the price, she's letting me stay. Bottle of whiskey to help her mellow. Tara never has gone to any program not having a white lady to boss her.

Back at her trailer a little grill standing in the weeds. I clean it, find a bag of charcoal, get the fire started with a dip of gas from the truck. Squat on the ground, knees cracking, waiting for it to die down, Little Squirt sits between my knees. Phone rings in the house trailer, Tara calls out Squirt's mama on her way to Oklahoma with some dude she met at the spa. I look at Squirt to see if he's crying, he's in a bag of chips stuffing his face.

Tara comes out to hang her laundry and I give her a sip from the bottle, she takes two more. Puts clothespins in her mouth, hanging sheets, she goes on about how "cute" I was a long time ago when we was close before she turned into Great-Aunt Tara. They don't call me Great-Uncle, though that's what I am. Sign of respect I guess.

Wet sheet on the line flaps in my face. "Was Grandpa your boyfriend?" Little Squirt asks her.

"Well we're kin—" I say.

"That don't necessarily stop it," Tara says shedding all kinds of smiles on me from her wrinkled-up face. I remember when her breasts put me in mind of two ripe pears under them thin shirts she wears. Has one of them on now but what it shows is different. She ruffles the hair what's left of it on top of my head. "You wouldn't believe how cute Old Grizzle Face was those days."

Now she's pinning up the biggest brazeer I ever seen, then these giant underpants. "Leave your ratty clothes out tonight I'll wash them for you fresh for the morning," she says.

"I don't want to put you to no trouble," I tell her, feeling which way the wind is blowing.

"No trouble at all, I got to put in another load of my own stuff."

I can just see them giant underpants circling around in the suds with my old jockeys and tore undershirt. "Let me think on it," I say though I don't hardly want to.

She's started up now and I guess there's no way to stop her, telling these foolish jokes about "the old days." Tells Squirt, "He used to sleep on the floor by my bed!"

"Why'd he do that?" Squirt asks, all big eyes.

"Only one bed in that old house," I tell him.

"Teehee! Wanted to be close to me I expect!" Tara says.

Well I seen it coming but what could I do. Grilled that steak the way I like it, well done with a good dressing of chile, we sit at her kitchen table eat every bit. I cut some small pieces for Squirt, pour Tara four shots of whiskey hoping she'll drowse off by the woodstove. No such luck. Whiskey just seem to perk her up. Squirt don't want to go to bed, I carry him in shove him down on his knees we say our prayers. He's praying for one thing I'm praying for another but the two go up together. Put him under the covers, switch off the light. Tara's bed big as the ocean next to his little bin. I'm hoping that's some protection.

"Just give me a blanket, I'll stretch out here by the stove," I tell her.

"I don't call that hospitality," she says. "My bed's plenty big enough for two."

"I don't sleep in no strange beds."

"I'm not going to touch you, scaredy-cat. Can't have you sleeping on the floor like them old days."

We went back and forth that way for a while. I pour her another shot.

"You not going to knock me out with this whiskey that's what you're thinking," she says.

"You always did have some kind of iron head for alcohol," I tell her.

She goes off about all the partying we done. I remember it well, she gets me to laughing. "Seems like nobody around here has that kind of fun anymore," she says sitting back in her chair propping her feet up on my knees.

"Well we're all old now," I say. Her feet on my knees in her pretty little shoes I leave them lay.

It gets to be late—I don't say nothing about it but Tara goes to yawning, says it's time to turn in. I don't ask no more about the blanket by the stove, follow her in her room, get undressed in the dark, don't want to wake up Georgie. It's a good thing we don't turn on the light see what time has done.

She crawls in first holds the covers open, I slide in by her, Georgie snuffling in his nose a foot away. "We got to be quiet," she says.

"I don't plan on a commotion," I tell her, feel her warm hand on my belly, so long since anybody touched me there. "I'm old, " I tell her.

"Old but seems like still hot to trot," she says, handling the evidence.

This has been coming a long time, somehow it's sweeter because of the wait. I have the memory of my girl cousin with the pear breasts that's way in the past, I can still feel it. She don't ask anything of me, just lay in her arms and let her squeeze me and some little piece of life comes back into me and she giggles and opens up. "Well well well," she says and I let go of a howl. She pushes the pillow down on my face, Georgie don't stir. Then we both go down in that deep sleep never is caused by anything else.

Georgie wakes up early, a little light seeping in the window, climbs up on the bed crawls over me and gets down between us. Tara throws her free arm over him, her hand lands on my chest. Warm, still warm. Georgie burrows down.

JULY FOURTH

July Fourth come round and the state banned all fireworks, took down the big tent by the highway where we always sold them, said the tribal cops would be watching.

"It's this drought," Daddy Cowboy told us. "We's all got the day off so let's go down to the City and look around."

More than a hundred miles south and ordinarily he won't waste the diesel but I guess he didn't want us kids hanging around with nothing to do. He told us to be ready, my cousin Tara, Jimmy-James her little brother, and me they call Sure Enough if I don't stop them.

We got up early, washed, dressed, waited by the door for Daddy to come by with his big red truck. He don't live with us no more after the last fight with Mama. She was sleeping late knowing we was off her hands. Already fearsome hot, that dust wind starting, the sun looking like a big red blister on the east edge of the sky, getting ready to cook us all day.

Daddy come roaring up in his truck and we run out. He had Aunt Your Mean Horse riding shotgun, not my favorite of the aunties but so what.

"Never was this hot till the government started monkeying with the weather," Daddy said. Tara and me knowed to stay quiet. No use asking him questions once he started down that road.

We'd got in the back quick before Daddy got pissed and changed his mind. He could do that if one of us kids was too slow getting in or tried to come barefoot. We wedged Jimmy-James between us, him already squalling.

"Shut that kid up before I drop you all the side of the road," Daddy said.

Tara come prepared with a piece of gum she shoved in the kid's mouth. Took him a while to chew and swallow it.

Aunt Your Mean Horse hung her big moon face over the seat. "Where's them seat belts?"

"I cut them out a while back, fixed that damn beep," Daddy said, pulling out onto the highway past the fireworks tent laying on its side like a big busted balloon. Not many cars this early on the holiday, only a big eighteen-wheeler hauling hay up from Colorado. Drought took all ours. "Price of hay going to kill me," Daddy said, flying by.

"You ask me it's time you got rid of all them horses," Aunt Your Mean Horse said, "now you too old and busted up to ride rodeo."

"Nobody asked you," Daddy said.

Aunt kept her big face hanging over the seat, black eyes a pair of searchlights. "You kids better mind yourself," she said, her voice deep from whiskey and cigarettes. She's Mama's sister not Daddy's and they never have seen eye to eye but he had to go live with her after Mama kicked him out. She was married sometime back to Uncle Thrash then he run off and left her 'cause she never made no babies. She couldn't find nobody else. That story got around.

We parked in one of them lots with about a thousand spaces, got out, commenced to walk around the City. Daddy spied somebody he knowed from way back laying under a tree. "How you doing old man?" he said, went to sit with him and smoke.

Auntie hoisted Jimmy-James asleep on her shoulder, told Tara and me to keep close. She commenced to walk down the sidewalk. In a minute here come Daddy. "Worst drunk I know," he said. "I guess they finally threw him out back home."

Well that city's a big place, streets and streets, all kinds of shops, but friendly-seeming 'cause there's more of us there than any other city, between the university, the streets, and the jail. We looked at everything and

Tara started fussing to go in one of the jewelry shops but one look from Auntie shut her up fast. I didn't see nothing I had to look at close up.

Pretty soon it was eat time and Jimmy-James woke up fussing but Tara had a bottle in her purse, she took him started feeding him before Daddy could say a word. Daddy turned into a place he knowed, got us out, sized us up and made me tuck in my shirttail, swiped a dried bugger off Tara's cheek. Auntie pulled herself up like she mattered too.

It was cool in that place with the AC running and six of us sitting at the big table, a few more at the counter. I seen pie slices runny with filling in the case behind the counter and some guy was frying up burgers.

Daddy made us speak to the men he knew which was most at the big table. Then he set us at another table and went up to order Green Chile Chicken Stew for everybody like he always does. "If you don't like it you can pay for something else." I like green chile but my first spoonful was so hot with chile it just about choked me and I put my napkin over my mouth so Daddy wouldn't see. Tara took one sniff of hers, pushed back from the table. Daddy was shoveling the stew down like there was no tomorrow and Auntie was making a good run at it too.

"Box it up," Daddy told the guy waiting on us. "That'll be your supper." But Tara and I knew he'd forget it by the time we got home. It'd lay in the back of his truck till it rotted.

Tara said, "Jimmy-James needs changing bad." We could smell him.

"Take him to the bathroom quick," Daddy said and Tara did.

"Why you made all these kids," Auntie said in her tired voice.

"I only made four of them so far," Daddy said. "Have to make some more since you won't."

She was heating up. "You think that's what I wanted?"

"Well, far as I know, Thrash is—"

"Nothing to do with Thrash," she cut him off. "IHS got me when I was fifteen, took everything out."

"Why you?"

"I'm a full blood, that's what they was looking for. Did more than a thousand of us I heard."

"Thrash know that?"

"I didn't know myself for sure."

"Well time told," he said.

"It sure did." Her voice was like sucking lemon.

Then Tara come back with Jimmy-James cleaned up and Daddy paid and we went out of there, didn't even wait for the guy with the takeout boxes.

We stopped at a coffee place so Auntie and Daddy could fill up and when he paid I saw Daddy had a big roll of bills in his front pocket. Never did carry a wallet, charge card, or most times not even his license. "I'll look back home for it," he'd say if he got stopped. Most likely it was out of date or suspended. Tribal cops didn't make much of a fuss, state cops something different.

Daddy took us to this museum place, shelves of our old things, pots and such, so many I couldn't hardly see them all. Daddy didn't like the smell of it, said real low they was all stole. White women everywhere trying to explain the pots to us.

Auntie took out a sage smudge stick, lighted it, waved it 'round till a white lady said it was against the rules but by then the good sage smell was all around us. Some beeping started and Auntie had to go outside and bury the smudge stick in the dirt.

Daddy had just about had it. He hustled us out. Jimmy-James was fussing again and Tara put her finger in his mouth for him to suck on. That worked for a while.

Heading for the truck I saw a big sign nailed to a post: Site of Clifford Indian Boarding School 1879–1960.

"Was that where they sent...they took the kids?" Tara said.

Auntie said, "They got me when I was eight. I stayed there four years. We did all the cooking and cleaning for the nuns and then they put us out to service. The boys had to cut off their hair and take care of the cattle, some of them run off fast."

"You learnt reading and writing," Daddy said, wiping his sweaty face with his bandanna. "The monks at my place taught us boys all those old books nobody speaks about anymore but I keep a lot of them in my mind."

Auntie didn't argue. I could see she had another opinion.

"Did the kids want to go?" Tara asked, jiggling Jimmy-James on her arm, looking up at Daddy.

"Hell no, didn't have no choice," he said. "My place was up near the Yellowstone, run by these monks. Do something wrong they beat you. Do something right they beat you. I run off the first year."

"I went right here," Auntie said, "great big school. Learned to crochet and make biscuits. Every winter a fair number of us died. Used to be a graveyard here." We was standing in the parking lot.

"Still here only they cemented it over," Daddy said.

"Well that does seem a shame. Families never knew?"

"How they going to find out way up on the reservation? Didn't have no phones back then, no way to get here to see."

"I knowed one of them that died," Auntie said. "My baby brother."

"That must of been way back in time," Daddy said.

"Well it was but still. It was a cold winter, he coughed all night in that freezing room with all the beds. I went and laid with him to warm him but some sister come and yanked me out. He was gone by breakfast time. They put him down in the dirt before I knowed what happened."

Daddy looked at her and I saw something you don't see too often with Daddy Cowboy. It seemed like maybe he was sorry. "You all wait here," he said, and he went to his truck and opened the back and I saw the welter of his tools. He pulled out a pickax. "Come on," he said, and went to the middle of the parking lot, only a few cars baking in the sun. "Tell me where," he said to Auntie.

She commenced pacing, looking down. Stopped here, stopped there. After a while she said, "Here," pointing down.

Daddy went to where she was, pickax hefted. She pointed and he drove the ax down hard on the spot, six times until a big piece of cement broke up. "Get them pieces out," he said, and Tara and me kneeled down, started picking. We opened up a hole two feet wide, orange clay at the bottom.

"All right go to it," Daddy said. Auntie went down on her old creaking knees by the hole. She put her face right to it. That hot wind blew up her skirt. I didn't get no pleasure out of seeing her big white bloomers, fat thighs straining.

Tara pulled her skirt down.

Auntie started to say some of the old words nobody knows no more. Sounded almost like singing or praying. Far as I could tell she said the same words over and over. Daddy was watching her with the stare he gets when he sees a flock of wild turkeys in what's left of his corn.

Auntie fished a little pot out of her pocket, let some drops fall in the hole all the time saying her words. Then she made the sign of the cross and hoisted herself up. "Fill the hole," she told us.

Tara and I scrambled the pieces back in. "How they going to breathe down there?" Tara said.

"They quit breathing a long time ago," Daddy said.

Auntie made the sign of the cross one more time said one of the church prayers. Daddy chimed in. Tara and I don't know none of them words. Mama is against it.

Daddy said, "Tell them to rest in peace. Kids like you."

Tara said, "Rest in peace." I said it too after Tara bumped me in the side.

Then Jimmy-James went to squalling again and we all piled in the truck for the long ride home.

Aunt Your Mean Horse couldn't let it go. She come to me a week later, asked me to drive her down there again. "You got your permit?"

"Yes, ma'am," I said, which was a lie. Daddy Cowboy didn't have time or patience to take me for the test but sometimes you have to lie to get something done. I been driving everything with four wheels, ATVs, trucks, sedans, cement trucks, since I turned eight.

"Well get ready to take me tomorrow, early. You can drive my Chevy," she said. "I don't drive no more. Now I'm half blind."

I never had noticed that. Seemed to me she had eyes in the back of her head but anyway. It may be she wanted company.

"And don't you go speeding and get us stopped," she said like I was that kind of fool.

So we drove that long hot drive to the City in her old rusted-out Chevy. It turned out she'd made an appointment with somebody at that museum. He was waiting for us, big fat white man in a suit and tie like the heat never bothered him. AC running full blast in his office anyway. He started out all friendly. "What can I do for you folks?" But he was looking at us like we was some spoiled piece of meat.

"They's kids buried under that parking lot of yours," Auntie said. "I want them dug up."

"Well now that may be so but all that's a long time ago, nothing left by now."

"They's bones left," she said, "and their folks want them back to bury right."

"That's government property, I don't have the authority—"

"Then who do?" Auntie was hanging her big white moon face over him and I saw him lean back to get away.

"You need to get in touch with D.C. to answer that question," he said. "And now if you'll excuse me."

I thought for sure that would stop Auntie in her tracks but no such thing. She told me, "Drive me to this here address" which turned out to be the office of the City paper. When we got there she told me to go find somewhere to park in the shade. I took time to get me a Pepsi and some chips and when I come back for her waiting on the sidewalk she was grinning. "Didn't want to talk to me but changed they minds fast," she told me. "Now take me home."

Few days later paper run this big story, Where Are All the Lost Children? It weren't a week before somebody from D.C. called the fat man and he had to call Auntie to make another appointment.

"Well you sure have made enough trouble," he said when we come in the door.

"Not yet," she said. "What're they saying they'll do?"

"They ain't going to dig up my parking lot—"

"Stop right there," she said. I could feel her heat right through the sleeve of my shirt.

"Now wait a minute before you get all het up. They're going to put up a plaque.

He reached for a paper. "Solid bronze, last forever. They want you to approve the words. 'Under this parking lot untold numbers of Native children are buried. This plaque honors their lives and asks their survivors to forgive the past.'"

Then it was quiet for a while in that office with the AC roaring.

Auntie said, "I'll have to think about it. My baby brother's under there."

"Well I'm sure sorry for your loss," the fat man said.

"His granma is still with us. Still cries for him. She'll want to bury him proper."

"Nobody is going to dig up my parking lot," the fat man said. "Why at times like when the balloon fiesta is going we have five hundred cars out there."

"Driving over those kids without even knowing it."

"They'll know it now with this plaque," the fat man said and I knew it was the best we was going to do.

Turned out Auntie Your Mean Horse knew that too though it took her a while. The next Native American Day she asked me to drive her down to the City again and when we got to that parking lot, she saw that piece of bronze nailed up on a thick metal post and the whole base of it was jammed with make-believe flowers.

COWBOY AND THE WHITE LADY

That winter I was dating this white lady I liked more than most I've had. She was sweet, never threw a fit about socks on the floor. Maybelle. She had this grown son, kid named Tommy, living with her for months till she couldn't take it anymore and sent him off to roost at the shelter which was wrong to my way of thinking 'cause kid had all kinds of money from his long-gone dad.

Well she got agitated that December (women get crazy with Christmas coming), told Tommy he needed a job and asked me—I was living with her off and on at the time—could I do something about Tommy, sleeping all day, out all night, the usual. I raised three boys of my own, wild as coyotes, got all them bolted down to making a living so it made sense for me to try. Tommy dropped out of some college, never worked a job in his life, so getting him bolted down was going to take some doing.

I was working construction, doing finish work, carpentry and that, on this fine big house in the mountains, so I told her, "I'll take him on the job tomorrow if you can get him up and moving by eight a.m."

That didn't seem likely from what I'd seen, Tommy falling out of bed around four in old PJ bottoms, scratching his naked belly and ordering coffee from his mom like she was a wayside diner, but somehow or another she got him up and he was sitting on the couch with his coffee when I come by at eight.

"Your mom tells me you want to work," I said. Tommy didn't say nothing, just went on snuffling up his coffee, finally put the cup down and got up.

Mom comes in, kisses him like she's never going to see him again, tells him she's proud. "Get your jacket, it's cold today," she tells him, then goes to dig out gloves and a wool hat he won't wear 'cause it makes him look like a clown.

Kid follows me out to my truck, getting ready to ride shotgun till I tell him to take himself to the back seat. Shotgun is Jose's seat, the best plasterer I know.

I drive off as soon as he's in, thinking to hear Mom shouting about seatbelts which my truck don't have 'cause I shut off the beep and cut them loose. I go to pick up Jose on the south side of town in one of them big new developments for poor people.

Jose gets up front, a big guy always ready for whatever, turns around to say hello to the kid. Turns back around.

"He's on the floor."

I look over my shoulder. Sure enough the kid's curled up on the floor.

I don't say nothing, drive out north to the construction site.

We are late. Work has already started.

Jose gets out, looking a little weird. "He here to work?"

"Only way I'd bring him—" But kid is still on the floor.

I get out, open the back door, tell him to get out, but he just pushes his face in his knees.

I say it again, still nothing.

I reach in and grab a good hank of that yellow hair.

"Ouch!" he yells, falls like a bag of potatoes out of the truck flat on the ground. Gets to his feet, scrape on his chin. Jose is staring.

"Get that broom and sweep," I tell Tommy. Leaves everywhere. Kid looks at me like nobody ever give him an order and it's some kind of insult. Bends down and lays his hand on the broom. Don't pick it up.

"What's wrong with him?" Jose asks me. Six of his own and every one of them a worker since they could walk.

"Too much mom."

But it isn't just mom.

"He on something?" Jose asks, watching him raise up the broom like it weighs fifty pounds.

"Sure is," I say. "Mom don't know nothing about it."

"You going to tell her?" Jose and I were close then, sometimes spent a night together.

"No," I tell him. "She'd freak. Seems like he just smokes weed most nights, why he can't get up in the morning, but his mom's kind of person thinks weed's heroin." I've smelled weed on Tommy every time I see him, same as now.

Kid still standing there and I tell him to get started sweeping, I go on inside to work on the paneling I'm putting in the "library," special room for the owner's books on some war, leather and gold sets. Needs lot of shelves over my walnut paneling, screws ruining the good wood but that's what he wants.

Working, I forget about Tommy. I been in enough trouble in my time and my kids the same, found out long since words don't mean nothing. Bad apples got to nearly die more than once before they decide to quit if they ever do.

I go outside to eat my lunch, don't see nothing of the kid, broom laying on the leaves.

I sit down on the wall with Jose and he gives me one of his wife's enchiladas she always makes. Good, too. I tell him must be worth being married to get a good lunch regular.

After a while here comes Tommy looking like a starved wolf.

"Where's your lunch?" I go.

"Mom didn't fix me anything."

"You can't put two pieces of bread and a slice of lunch meat together?"

He shrugs.

Jose starts to give him the last enchilada. I say, "He gets hungry enough he'll bring lunch." Jose puts the enchilada back in his lunch pail.

So the starved wolf sits on the ground, watches us eat.

When we're done, I tell Tommy to pick up the broom. "That's your job, sweep up those leaves."

"Didn't sleep last night, got to take a little nap in your truck."

"Not on my time you don't. Get to work."

He picks up the broom and starts sweeping up little humps of leaves. Jose goes back to his plastering. I go in to ruin the rest of my walnut paneling.

Work day ends at four p.m. Jose and I walk to my truck. No sign of Tommy, and some leaves still laying around. I sound the horn and here he comes around the side of the house like he's been over there taking a nap.

"I swept a lot of leaves," he tells me. This time he takes his place in the back. I think, Well that's something. Not much but something.

I drive back to his mom's. I stop, he gets out, I tell him, "Eight a.m. tomorrow."

He starts to say something. I drive off.

Later Mom—Maybelle—calls me all over me with thanks like I hung the moon. "How'd you get him to work?"

"Told him what to do and he did it after a while."

"He never listens to me."

"Well, you're his mom."

"He used to listen."

"He's grown now or trying to be."

Then I hear these big choking sobs, not the first time. "He makes me so sad. What did I do wrong?"

"Maybe nothing," I tell her. "All boys go through this some time or another, looks like they can't grow up without it. Anyway he don't make you sad."

"What're you talking about?" She stops sobbing.

I remember some line from a meeting. "Nobody makes you feel what you don't want to feel." The sobbing starts again and I hang up.

I heard and believed a few things like that, court ordered to go to meetings after my last DUI. The first rule, stop the blame game. You did it to yourself, nobody else.

I'd like to know what happened to Tommy's father. These kids seem sprung whole but there's something left out.

He's not ready or anywhere near it when I come to pick him up next morning. Standing in the kitchen in his PJ bottoms with his little skinny belly hanging out.

"I can't wait for you," I tell him, but I do, get him to dress and make a cheese sandwich and find a bag to put it in.

Jose waiting in the truck shaking his head. "Don't say nothing," I say. "He's trying."

I get to sort of like the son of a gun by Friday when I hand him his paycheck. He looks at it like it's the first money he's ever seen.

Monday rolls around and I know what to expect. No Tommy when I come to pick him up. His mom claims he needs his sleep.

"Out late," I say, not a question.

"Not only that he brought a bottle of whiskey home and drank the whole thing." She's standing in the door in a ratty old robe, looks like she can use some sleep herself. A pretty woman but she's getting old.

"That's where a good portion of his first week's pay went. I'll get him up," I say, starting for the stairs. She tries to block me with her skinny arm but I walk on through and up, guessing the first door at the top is the one. Sure enough there's Tommy lying zonked on the bed in his jockeys.

"Get up, I need you on the job." Not a word so I grab his arm and pull him down on the floor. He don't weigh more than a powder puff. "You work for me, you work for me," I say.

He wakes up, starts to crawl to his work clothes on a chair. I throw them at him, he sits up starts dressing. Whining but I don't pay that no mind. I herd him out to the truck where Jose is waiting and shove him in the back. "Don't go back to sleep. I don't plan to wake you up again 'less it's with a bullet to your head."

When we get to the job he falls out of the truck, skins his elbow and starts whining. I stick the broom in his hand. Jose and I go to our jobs inside and out and I don't hear nothing from Tommy till noon. Then he comes and goes to bitching 'cause he didn't bring lunch and I let Jose hand him one of his wife's bean burritos, the best, with a good dollop of red-hot green chile. Chile burns Tommy's mouth and he going to start the organ going again but this time I shut him up with one look. He's learning. Ate, drank, shut up, and went back to sweeping, time of year leaves come down every night.

Job would have gone on like that but then his mom goes crazy. Tommy brought whiskey home again, threw up all over his room, wouldn't clean up the mess, and she had to call in a service. Well, that was the last straw.

She's waiting for me next morning in that ratty old robe looking like some witch. "I'm taking steps," she says. "You're too rough with him, I saw how you dragged him out of bed."

"Sometimes—" I start but she drowns me out.

"Nobody handles my son that way!"

"You want me to quit just tell me," I say.

"Yes, quit!" she screeches. "I've arranged for him to go somewhere!"

"Somewhere?"

"To get the help he needs!" She's close to me now and she smells like burnt toast, I wonder why.

"He'll never go," I say.

"Not up to him! I've arranged his transportation." She swipes a few tears off her cheek. "This place in Wisconsin. They'll know how to help him, they do it all the time. Best recommendations!"

I don't stop to ask anything more but I'm pissed.

That was the end of Tommy for me. Next day when I come to pick him up, Maybelle tells me he's gone. She hired two goons with handcuffs, dragged him out of bed at three a.m. and drove him to the airport. I guess they took the handcuffs off before they loaded him on the plane but I don't know. No phone calls allowed for the first month, not that I plan to call him.

Early that January, Jose and I finish our work on the fine big house in the mountains but with the amount of construction going on here we both found more work the next week. Rich people from Dallas flooding in 'cause our town is cute and we got good weather all year round.

An open winter, no snow so no need to pause construction. In the old days we laid off January and February but not no more which is good for contractors and the rich folks moving in. They used to have to wait till spring for their houses to be ready but not now. Somebody around here always carrying a sign going on about "climate change" but for us in construction it's nothing but good.

First of March, Maybelle calls me with those big sobs. It seems like Tommy run off from the place in Wisconsin and ended up overdosing in a tramp camp by the tracks.

Jose crosses himself when I tell him, says he'll ask the priest to say a novena.

"He'll need it," I say and just about believe it. If I was a praying man I'd say something for him too but I ain't a praying man, never have been and never will be.

Maybelle gets what's left of Tommy flown back, plans a funeral in the cathedral though far as I know neither one of them ever went to Mass but a big donation makes a difference.

"I need you to come," she tells me, sobbing big-time. "You're the closest thing he had to a dad."

"Not that close," I say. "Where's the real one?"

"I couldn't locate him, maybe just as well. You got a black suit?"

"I'll scramble up something."

I did, too, surprised myself. I kept seeing that kid's skinny belly hanging out of his old PJ bottoms. My boys never went down that far. What the program calls Hitting

Bottom kills most of them, none of mine and I'm grateful.

Gratitude only takes me so far when I see Maybelle waiting for me on the cathedral steps, all black and a veil too. "Mom or widow?" I ask hoping to rouse a smile but she just hitches on to my arm. I don't see no choice but to walk her in.

Cathedral organ is blowing up a storm and all these white people in the pews turn their heads to look at us, closest thing to a wedding I'll ever see. Maybelle's hand is gripped on my arm and I feel her trembling.

I want to stop in a back pew but she more or less drags me to the front. She don't have nobody, no sister aunt or cousin to plane in and have the tissues ready.

I don't carry no tissues and Maybelle ends up wiping her tears on her sleeve.

The priest starts his long litany and the people around me don't know what to say. I find the page in the prayer book and pass it back to the woman behind me. I know the words, taught by the Jesuits a long time ago and been to many funerals.

Priest ends with the dust to dust and then the incense and the choir and everybody crowds to the door. Some of the women stop to give Maybelle a kiss and then we're all out in the sunshine.

"We're going across the street to the hotel, I've arranged a buffet," she tells me and that's where I draw the line.

"Sorry but not me, I got to feed my horses."

I have to pry her fingers off my arm.

"You'll call me later?" she says and I nod and say something, not sure afterwards what but I know it's not a promise and I also know it don't matter because she'll call me.

She did that evening, said we had a sacred connection now 'cause of me being at the funeral. I never had figured on that. Said she wanted me to help her chose Tommy's marker, didn't want his grave lying all bare and desolate with nothing on top.

"I'm not one for spending time on the dead," I told her. "What's gone is gone."

"He admired you so much, told me once he wanted to grow up to be a man like you."

"Not much chance with you barging in."

"Just do this one more thing for me and I'll leave you alone."

I ended up driving her to this monument place on the north side of town, all kinds of crosses and so forth to choose from. She wanted me to choose but I told her it wasn't my thing. Long time later after walking back and forth and saying this and that and asking the man for prices she bought this cross she'd seen right at the start. Hell of a lot of money for a big lump of gray stone but that's what she wanted. Then arranging to have it carted over to the cemetery and stuck in the ground. Another pretty penny.

I drove her back to her place, went in to have a cup of coffee. I didn't feel like I could say no to that.

"We can work something out, I know we can, we been through so much together," she says, pouring me a big cup. "You want cream and sugar?"

"No."

She tried a smile. "No to what?"

"Cream and sugar. I always take black." Seemed to me she might have known that.

"What about the other?"

"You need to get over this before you ask me."

"But I love you," she said.

How many times, I wanted to say but didn't. How many times, I thought, have I heard those words in going on fifty years. And they mean them, they surely do. But then when it comes down to dirty dishes in the sink and who's going to drive the kid to school, that's a whole different matter. That's when I always start to hear about "my own life," "my independence," "my dreams." Well, they have a right to that, we all do. But as soon as they start, I think about Jose waiting in the truck with his wife's burritos, the best in town with a big dollop of red-hot green chile.

"I'll think on it," I said and meant it just as surely.

TELLING THE TRUTH

After he'd been with Ruth more or less a year she started looking at Cowboy funny and first he thought let sleeping dogs lie. But it got to bothering him and he tried his usual fixes, some ripe jokes and a few kisses but she swatted them away.

She called him to meet for lunch—she didn't give him a way out—at his favorite place, the café where Raoul his new young friend worked. That was more than a part of the reason Cowboy liked to go to the café in spite of what it was called, True West and Then Some. The West was full of these tourist places and usually he steered clear of them and the concho belts riding fat bellies but he wanted to see Raoul and catch another one of his smiles so he told her he'd go. This was five years after he finally left the rez and moved to the city for a good job in construction.

At the café they sat at his usual corner table and ordered his usual, fish tacos with green chile. Raoul served them but ran off without giving Cowboy his smile.

Cowboy felt Ruth watching him. "You really light up for that boy," she said in her plain voice.

"He's a good-looking kid. I like his earrings." Two little white daisies, one in each ear.

"I wish you'd light up like that for me," she said still in that plain voice. She knew Cowboy didn't stand for scenes. He'd up and left a few times when she was throwing one, she'd beg him to come back.

"What's it mean, earrings in both ears?" she asked. "I know one in the left means gay, or is it the right..."

Cowboy let that go.

The next thing she said sounded like it'd been waiting in her mouth at least a month. "Isn't that who you really want?"

Cowboy went on chewing. "You mean little Raoul?"

"Well, the way you look at him—"

"You think I want him to screw me in the butt?"

"Or something," she said, looking at her plate. She wasn't eating.

"I'm not thinking about it," he told her.

Then she gave him one of her sayings. "It's so important to acknowledge our hidden desires." He'd heard that more than a few times.

"Tell me yours," he said though he really didn't need

to know. "You want some girlie to suck your titties?"

"No," she said. "And never have. Wanted that, I mean."

"What about that time you was thirteen and spent the night with that redhead? You told me how you ground on her."

"I knew right away it was a terrible mistake. She never spoke to me again."

"Then why you trying to get after me about Raoul?"

"Well you don't want me anymore so I wondered." There were tears in her voice now but she knew better than to let them run. Cowboy didn't tolerate tears. A while ago she'd said, "If you don't like women's tears why do you make them happen?" He'd walked out and stayed away a week.

"I want you to tell me the truth," she said, and stuck her fork in her taco.

Sometimes she got that in her voice, that steel, and then he knew it was no use to argue. "I'm tired," he told her. "I'm sixty-seven years old."

"You didn't used to be tired," she said.

Cowboy never had understood why women were so hung up on doing the same thing over and over. Not that he didn't enjoy it but doing it over and over week in, week out kind of took the juice out. "Let's go back to your place and we'll do it right now," he said.

"I have a dentist appointment at three."

"It won't take that long," he said.

"You're right about that. I never have been able to get you to do foreplay."

That word again. It always made him think of the way the pitcher warms up before his first throw.

He'd stopped eating now although he loved fish tacos and green chile. Somehow she's driven him into a corner—she'd been trying to do it for a long time—and he resented it like hell. "If you're not satisfied—"

"I'm not giving up." She cut him off with that steel.

"Well then what?"

"Maybe if we get Raoul in bed—"

"Don't get started," he said.

"I'll do anything I need to if it'll get you going again."

He knew she meant it. He also knew he wouldn't be able to come back to the café.

Raoul thought they were finished and took their plates, food hardly half eaten. Cowboy didn't have the energy to tell him to wait.

"You owe me for haying the north field," he said.

They always got into money around then. She had a lot, more than he could imagine, and sometimes she paid him for his work at the ranch and sometimes she didn't. He knew the paying or not paying was tied to bed but that was the last thing he was going to talk about.

"I can't afford it this month," she told him, a bald-faced lie—he hadn't even named what she owed, waiting to see how close he could come to doubling it. She had so much it surely couldn't matter and anyway she never tried to find out the usual rate. "I just paid for your tractor and that's all I can afford till my next installment."

He wondered how a more than grown woman—she was seventy-seven—lived with an allowance doled out from some bank in New York but he guessed since she hadn't earned a penny of it (somebody back in her family made a killing off oil) she had to put up with the terms. Still, he was irked and lost hold of himself and asked her how she could stand having her money paid out that way.

"That's the way it's set up in the trust," she told him like she'd done a million times before.

"Go to court, get it changed."

"Nobody in the family likes me and if I did that they'd hate me and Mom's ninety-one and I'm counting on her will."

"Is that going to come in installments too?" he asked like he didn't know the answer.

"If she leaves me anything."

"You mean I'm going to have to wait to get paid till some old lady dies?"

She jumped up from the table, banging it with her knees. "I won't listen to this," she said and he saw that steel flash in her eyes.

"Well then just tell me when you plan on paying me."

"I'm going to put the ranch on the market you keep on this way." She'd said that a few times. A year ago she'd called it "our ranch" although her name was the only one on the deed and he knew pretty well what that meant, but that was when they were new together and even talked a few times about living on that godforsaken piece of high mesa he'd told her not to buy.

She got a hold of herself. "First of next month," she told him. "How much?"

"That's three weeks off. I owe on my mortgage." Cowboy still lived mostly in his own house in town, nothing to brag about but at least his.

"That's not my responsibility," she said and gave herself a little shake and sat down at the table again. Raoul had been watching and came to see if they wanted coffee. She wouldn't say so Cowboy ordered for both, with sugar and cream ("and not those little plastic pots"). With prices going sky-high due to the war even the True West had cut out real cream.

Raoul promised the real thing and when he looked up at him, Cowboy saw something in his eyes he never had seen before and surmised Raoul had heard what Ruth was suggesting.

Raoul was on borrowed time with no papers and the country was getting mean about illegals and he knew Ruth with her connections—her brother was some kind of big politician—could have cleaned up the situation but he'd be skinned before he asked her to help Raoul now. She had too much of a hold already because of the ranch and the money he needed for his mortgage and helping Raoul would tighten her grip.

The coffee when it came was too hot. Ruth looked at her watch—she still wore one—and he knew she was thinking about the dentist. She'd lost four of her lower teeth and when she laughed there was a big gap she wanted the dentist to fill in. She'd told Cowboy it was going to cost her almost a thousand dollars and he'd made the mistake of asking her to put the teeth off and pay him what she owed and that talk had not ended well.

"I can't help wondering how you managed before we met," she said, using her plain voice that never had tears in it. "There were a lot of years when you had the kids and your house and your horses and as far as I know you never did work." She picked up her coffee cup and took a sip but it was still too hot and she set it back down.

"I worked plenty in construction till it dried up," he said. "After that nuclear place up on the hill blew up rich people quit coming and they's the ones want the big new houses."

Ruth had nothing to say to that. She'd carried a sign a few times against that business, tried to get him to carry a sign too but he wouldn't because at first it just meant a lot of jobs.

He knew she liked plenty of sugar so to buy some time and change her tone he poured a lot in her cup and even picked up a spoon and stirred it for her. He stirred in some cream too to cool it.

She watched him do it but she didn't thank him, which showed how far off the path they'd come because ordinarily she had her manners. But she did take a sip.

"At the time I also had Moira." He didn't ordinarily go there but something about her plain voice told him he had to now just to irk her a little.

"Did that poor woman pay for everything?"

He fired up in spite of himself. "Moira was not a poor woman, she was my wife and the mother of my children."

"Did she divorce you when she got sick of paying?"

"I divorced her," he said. Ruth knew that, she was just trying to spite him. "Money had nothing to do with it." He could feel her grip tightening.

"I never have understood why you didn't get alimony. You still had Bobby living with you."

"Court always favors the mom," he said, "and Moira never had that much."

"Well she sure lives high on the hog now. I guess that's the new husband."

My God it was awful and he was sorely tempted to get up and leave for good this time but he needed to pay on his mortgage before the bank went ahead and foreclosed. He reached across the table and touched her hand which was stove-hot. She snatched it back. "Let's talk about this some other time," he said.

And then by God before he knew what she was doing she signaled to Raoul and thinking they wanted the bill he came over.

"We have a little idea we want to discuss with you," she said.

Cowboy tried to catch her eye and get her to shut up but she was focused on the boy.

"We need some help at our ranch," she said. "Just some chores and handyman stuff."

Raoul looked interested. "What're you going to pay?"

She named a good sum, above minimum, and as it turned out he worked pretty regular on the ranch that winter and Ruth had the sense not to get into anything else.

The weekend before Christmas, Ruth asked Cowboy over for breakfast at the ranch on Sunday, a big meal they used to have as a habit, bacon, scrambled eggs, toast, the whole works. They'd both enjoyed it then but it'd been a while because now she was living at the ranch and he was back in his house in town.

She knew he hated pancakes but she was fixing them when he came in and got distracted looking at him and burned a bunch. The smell filled up his nose and he turned off the burner and emptied the mess in the garbage and set the pan to soak. Ruth sat down like a lump in a kitchen chair, not overweight but heavy in the butt. Then she started her verse: "I gave you my heart and my body—"

"Well at least you didn't give me your soul," he said, already fired up.

"If I had, I wouldn't be here now."

"Where?"

"Hospital or graveyard."

Cowboy laughed. "That's a joke. You got so much soul, honey, you could've give me a big slice and still have plenty left."

"What—?"

"Your money, darlin'."

"That's not my soul," she said.

"You could have fooled me."

"Anyway I've been so generous!"

"Not enough and you know it. You have me always scraping just to get by."

She was tearing up now. "That's my fault?"

"Sure. I'm talking about money, sweet pants. What's heart and soul to that? I got to live, Ruth."

"When we were lovers—"

He cut her off. "What's that? A squirt."

"Don't you dare—"

"That's what it is. You don't want to hear it. Women never do. You want to go on about 'love.' I don't go on about 'love' 'cause it don't feed me let alone my horses and my dog."

"How much did you expect?"

"You don't get it." He was breathing hard. "You never

will get it. All that money comes to you like on the wings of angels and it goes that way too. You didn't make it. Some old guy back in your family made it. I've seen the way twenties drop off you for any panhandler sitting in the gutter. Fifties and more too. You never can know how my first dollar felt when Old Man Dixon paid me for shoveling his walk. So yes, you've been 'generous' so you can feel OK about dropping me flat. What's cock and cunt to that? What's love? Quit sniveling and tell me, I want to know."

"Oh you're brutal." Tears were running now.

"No I'm not. I'm just telling you what you don't want to hear."

"Does that make it the truth?"

"For me it does." He got up to refill his coffee cup but the pot was empty and scorching on the bottom. He turned off the switch and remembered when he'd been so crazy about her fancy coffee machine he'd run it two or three times a day and he didn't even like coffee that much.

Ruth got up and ran water in the sink, splashed her face. He could see she was trying to get a hold of herself and he did appreciate that but it was a little late. He was still hot from his head to his heels.

"I have an idea." Now it was her plain voice but a little warmer. "Let's go away next weekend, somewhere we can relax."

Cowboy wondered how he could find somebody to feed his horses and his dog. That excuse wouldn't mean anything to Ruth. She'd probably volunteer to send one of her "people"—those men scurrying around her house with rakes and brooms—but he didn't want any one of them fooling with his horses. "Where you want to go?" he asked.

"We've always had a good time in Truchas, and there's that little inn you enjoy."

He remembered a weekend the past year when they'd driven north into the mountains and the clear air had somehow seemed to help. "OK," he said, "I'll go with you." He still had to pay on his mortgage.

They drove up there the next weekend. The man at the front desk acted like he'd known them both since childhood and went to grinning like a fool and talking about the mountain view. Ruth signed in and when the man asked, "One key or two?" Cowboy said "Two," though where he was going to go in that godforsaken mountain town he didn't know and Ruth had the car.

She'd reserved something called the Bridal Suite though it didn't seem likely to Cowboy many brides ever stayed there. It was dark and the big bed took up almost all the space.

He threw his backpack on the bed. "Where's that mountain view the man promised?"

Ruth went to the window and pulled back the

curtains and sure enough there was Truchas Mountain big against the eastern sky and covered with new snow.

"Prettier than anything we see from the ranch," Ruth said, setting her suitcase on the rack.

"You fixing to move up here?"

She smiled, taking something white out and spreading it on the bed. "No," she said. "I just want us to enjoy the weekend. I brought your Christmas present."

Cowboy was already feeling sick and when she handed him a big box wrapped in shiny red paper the sick got worse. He didn't like presents, never gave them and almost never got any which was fine by him. Presents were just the way some women claimed their rights.

He laid the box on the bed beside his backpack. "I'll save this till Christmas."

"No," she said and she had that steel in her voice. "You open it right now," and she handed him scissors she'd packed on purpose.

There was no way around it and he cut the red ribbon and the red wrapping paper and opened the box. Inside a wad of thin paper he saw a leather jacket with suede on the elbows.

"Try it on," Ruth said. "I want to be sure it fits. It cost a lot."

"I bet it did"—probably enough, Cowboy thought, to pay what he owed. He pulled the jacket out and the smell of new leather filled the room and he saw the buffalo head buttons and the white silk lining. Before he knew it, Ruth was helping him put the jacket on and it fit like a glove, even the sleeves long enough.

There was a mirror hanging on the wall and she tugged him to it and he saw the jacket and his head rising up out of the leather collar. He hadn't shaved and his grizzle was gray and the hair hanging down over the leather collar was gray too. "Where in the name would I wear this," he muttered.

"Next time I take you to dinner at my club you won't need to be embarrassed."

Three months before she'd chosen that place for what was meant to be a celebration of their second year together. The guard at the gate wouldn't let him in till Ruth called him. The drive led up to a big building covered with lights and Cowboy was dazed by the glare and didn't see her waiting inside the glass door. After he'd wrenched the door handle a few times she fed a code into a box and the door opened on its own.

After that Cowboy was in no mood to enjoy the steak she ordered (it was tough as an old boot). She apologized for him being embarrassed, coming to that place in his work clothes. "I should have warned you," she said.

"These are the clothes I wear," he'd said in too loud a voice and people at the next table turned around to stare at him.

Now he pulled off the leather jacket. "I'm never going

to that place again," he said, "or any of the other places you like to go."

She made a hurt-little-girl face but then she said, "That doesn't matter to me, we'll just eat at our ranch."

"Our" again which meant nothing. This time he said it. "It's not our."

"Just because your name isn't on the deed—"

"And don't put that white thing on when you're fixing to go to bed!" he shouted. "I'm not getting in bed with you so make up your mind to that!" He was glad she couldn't know that seeing her nipples through that white might do something to him, something she wanted.

She let that pass, even his shouting. "Let's go downstairs and see what they have to eat," she said, and she folded the jacket and put it back in the box.

They ate some kind of dinner, Cowboy didn't really notice, and she told him a tale about the life she'd led before they met, New York, shopping, theatre—he knew the way it always went. He was glad she was doing the talking because he was having trouble choking down whatever was on his plate and he had no words anyway. Then he watched her eat a big slice of apple pie—her appetite never failed her—and when the bill came and he pulled out his wallet to pay in cash (he knew what the credit cards added) she laid her hot little hand on his wrist and stopped him. "I'm paying," she said and he couldn't do anything about it.

After dinner they sat in the bar a while and he knew better than to order a drink but she belted down a whiskey and smiled and clapped for some old fake cowboy strumming a guitar and singing a tune about rain. Then she got up and led the way to the stairs and Cowboy knew he had to follow her though he could never have said why. She had some kind of speed in her feet he had to keep up with. But when they got to the door of the Bridal Suite he pushed ahead of her with his key.

He got in the room first and sat on the bed. She went in the bathroom and ran a lot of water in the bathtub and sat in it and sang the tune about rain. He waited.

When she came out, he could see her whole body through the white thing and he lost hold of himself and grabbed her and laid her across his knees and pulled up the white thing and whammed her five or six times with the palm of his heavy right hand.

Her tail turned red and she looked around at him with tears in her eyes and she was smiling.

"You're finally doing what I want," she said. "It didn't even take Raoul. You want to spank me some more?"

He hit her a few more times. It was doing to him what she knew it would do.

In the morning she wrote him a check to pay off his entire mortgage.

COWBOY AND THE WEDDING

By August all the boys had went off to fight in Iran except my cousin Tara's son Johnny. He was sole support for little Josephina, Mom off somewhere far away and not likely to be found. Johnny had decent income working nights at the Crystal Cow, fancy place near the capitol, worked his way up to lead waiter on weekend nights, best tips. Daytimes he took care of Josephina.

I went with them one time to that climbing wall the City put up in the old tramp place by the tracks, watched that four-year-old Josie go up the wall, each little foot in one of the cups carved out for that purpose, Johnny standing guard but no more needed than a tree. I said, "Well ain't she the cute one!" He said, "Way more than cute."

We was friends from way back so it come as no real surprise when Tara told me Johnny wanted me for witness when he and Carlos got married, it now being legal in the state. She said it when we was in my truck lined up at Dunkin Donuts to get to the order window.

I looked at her.

"Don't give me that look, I know how you feel. It's time to move on now it's legal," Tara said. She was wearing that pink dress showing her full arms still with dimples in place of elbows though she's an elder now same as me.

"Legal don't make it natural," I said.

She started in on me then. Was it natural me having all those women, black, white, mixed, couldn't even remember their names? Natural—or right!—to throw kids out all over this part of the West and couldn't keep track of them and didn't particularly try?

"You don't know what you're talking about." I moved the truck one space up. "You want cinnamon?"

"You know I do, same as always."

"I send a wad of money to every single one of them moms soon as they ask and they ask pretty regular."

"Money ain't the same as being a father," Tara said. "I'm thinking about Old Jake Bear and your dad, rough as cobs but they stuck around."

"Not much choice," I said.

We was at the window. I ordered one cinnamon two jellies, paid, moved on to the next window to pick them up. "They's all growed anyways," I said. "Should be taking care of theyselves by now even if they ain't."

She calmed down then, taking a big bite of her cinnamon with sugar sprinkling down the front of her dress. She brushed it off.

"Do it for Johnny," she said. "You knowed him since forever."

"He asked?"

"Sure did. Won't have nobody for witness but you and Big Tom."

"That drunk," I said. "I need coffee to wash this thing down."

Tara didn't have time for me to get back in the line. "Tom went sober the same time Johnny did. They both just got their five-year medallions."

I knew then there wasn't no way out and ended up three weeks later under Tara's grape arbor. Green grapes one side still sour—I tried one—purple grapes other side sweet as cane sugar. I had my mouth crammed full when here come Judge Sandoval carrying his judge robe in a garment bag. I knowed him from court, always treated me fair. We shook hands.

"Where is everybody?" Sandoval asked. "I'm on a tight schedule, due in court."

"Tara's in the house fixing up Carlos and Johnny on the way, Big Tom with them. I called Tara on the cell phone to let her know to come quick."

"Johnny working regular?"

"Crystal Cow weekends, you seen the sign?"

"Never have been in there but I saw that sign," the judge said.

I never have been inside the Crystal either but most days I drive past the sign. Big glass cow (or something), all her veins lighted up showing red or blue milk (or something) running down her teats.

"Johnny doing all right with that little girl?" judge asked. "What's her name?"

"Josephina, goes up that wall the City put up by the tracks all the way to the top, no help. I seen her."

Judge don't say nothing 'cause here come Carlos and Johnny bright as shined pennies, black suits I knowed they'd bought special, polished black shoes thin as arrows. Big Tom hanging with them, some sort of bear man, works nights in the bakery then seems like he runs off to the woods to find his kind. He'd cleaned up some but don't look the better for it. Judge says hello like he's seen him too many times, hands shook all around.

Here come Tara flying from the house. She looks like a queen, white dress all the way to the ground with sparkles in it. Kisses Johnny loud on the cheek leaving a big red mark, tries to do the same with Carlos but he gets out of the way. Just nods at Big Tom.

"Lets get started," Johnny says. Carlos still hanging back, a little shy. Worked most days grilling hot dogs at the truck stop, better work than nothing but not by much.

Judge Sandoval slipped his black robe out of the garment bag, dropped it over his head, zipped it up and was ready to go. "Please stand facing each other," he said. Carlos and Johnny done that, Big Tom hovering at the back and Tara already crying, holding on to my arm. "I guess you not counting on any grandkids," I whispered and she give me a look would've killed a rattler.

Johnny was smiling at Carlos like he used to when he got up off the dirt in the school yard and the other kid was laid out crying.

The judge started to read from his papers. Oh they was a lot of promises, more than I ever heard, help and comfort in hard times, bringing out the best, understanding patience compassion. I wondered how them two men was going to keep all them promises in their heads.

"Now hold hands," the judge said and Johnny reached out and grabbed Carlos's hands and I thought seeing the side of his face how good-looking he was, all smooth black and white, could have had every girl in the county, probably did. Judge don't say nothing about how they was going to deal with the past, Carlos married a couple of times, kids all over, Johnny new to this change.

They hands was wedged together finger over finger till Judge Sandoval told them to get the rings and they turned loose and started digging in their pockets. Pulled out these little black drawstring bags. Johnny got his open first, Carlos came close to dropping his, then judge said to put them on and Carlos's did not go easy over his big knuckle but Johnny's went on smooth. I saw the gold glint.

"Now you are married," the judge said. "You may embrace." This was when the bride throws back her veil and tilts her face like a cup waiting to be filled but with Carlos and Johnny being more or less the same height it was grab and go. Tara was sobbing now to beat the band and kissed Johnny again, leaving another big red print on his cheek and I thought Carlos going to have his work cut out for him fending off this mom. She'll be over there every day with her green chile stew till Carlos has enough and throws her out if he's got the grit.

Big Tom was standing off to one side looking dazed as a heifer in the loading chute but now stepped up and shook hands offering congratulations. Then it was my turn. I shook both their hands hard looked at their rings, shook my head. "Them's the real thing!"

Here come little Josephina got away from whoever was in the house watching her, grabbed her daddy by the knees. I thought there's another one cuz soon as Carlos runs off Tara, here come Josephina. Johnny pulled her up in his arms and pushed her across to Carlos for a kiss. He was ready to do it but Josephina ducked her face in her daddy's suit shoulder so no go.

Seemed like the thing to do now was drink champagne. I had two bottles with me the best they sell at

Albertson's. Tara went in the house brought out some juice glasses. Johnny kind of looked at them like "What?" but then must of remembered Tara only has her tips from Kombo's Roadhouse other side of town. I went to taking off the wire around the top of a bottle but Johnny grabbed it away from me like only he knew how from opening champagne bottles every Saturday night at the Crystal Cow. The bottle got shook up in my truck and when he opened it champagne flew everywhere. Tara screamed, her dress soaked, sticking to her boobs. I guess we all looked away. Johnny poured, swiveling that bottle after each filling to cut off the drip.

Judge said he was working, couldn't accept champagne but would stay for the toasts and looked at me to get them started so I held up my juice glass and wished them a long and happy life. Then Tara got started about Johnny when he was a little kid, how the teachers fussed because he was "too silly," played with his food didn't get what was "appropriate," kids all wanted to touch his curls and he let them. "Always did love to be touched," Tara said.

Judge slid his robe off back in the garment bag, said goodbye. Johnny tried to hand him some bills, judge said he couldn't accept being a servant of the people. Said he runs some kind of bad boy summer camp and would welcome a tax-free donation. I heard myself say I'd chip in, didn't even think how that might help me next time

I stood in front of Judge Sandoval. Did think about that later though.

The judge took off, rest of us going to the Crystal Cow for lunch. I tried to beg off saying I had horses to ride but Johnny wasn't having none of that, said horses could wait for once. We divided ourselves into my truck and Johnny's shiny electric, Tara and Big Tom with me, Josephina with Carlos and Johnny. Tara tried to get her to ride with us, being Grandma for once, but that little girl had a mind of her own and went to ride with her daddy. "She's a stubborn little..." I said, almost putting in a bad word, "ain't she?" but Tara clouded up, said Josephina had a lot to deal with and was doing good.

We rode to the center of town, kind of drained of business now with Walmart, Costco, Trader Joe's out on the edge, so no problem finding parking spaces. Went inside the Crystal Cow, dark and cool in that place. Waiter friend of Johnny's had a special booth saved and we all squeezed in, Josephina on her daddy's lap. Took a while getting through those menus big as road signs. I had a time finding hamburgers, never had been in no place charged twenty-five dollars for a quarter pound of beef and a bun. Rest of them asked for salads which I guess was the right thing to eat for lunch but never had no appeal for me.

Food took a while coming, Josephina got restless, squirmed, started to bawl when Johnny wouldn't let her eat a butter ball plain. Tara tried to take her but little girl didn't seem to know her. I guess the grandma thing was new. "She's just tired and hungry," Tara said, like a four-year-old needed a reason for cutting up.

"Her ma coming back this way anytime soon?" I asked. I was just trying to fill up the gap before the food come but I guess it was the wrong thing. Everybody started staring at me like I'd made a bad smell.

"Josephina is going to be living with Carlos and me," Johnny said with that glare I used to see when I asked to copy his homework.

"You'd think her ma would want her, cute as she is," Tara said, reaching across to try to smooth out Josephina's hair. The girl jerked her head away.

I guess the champagne had kind of worked on Tara 'cause she turned to Carlos sitting next to her, said, "You OK living with a four-year-old?"

Carlos was getting his answer ready but Tara went right on. "Waking you up six a.m. weekends and holidays too? Sleeping in the bed between you two? I know how those girls are, raised a couple of them myself. They always run off my man."

Johnny said, "Cut it out, Ma" and here come the food.

I asked for well done but the hamburger was bloody. I didn't want to send it back and hold things up. Josephina was on a tear, got a hold of a butter ball, smeared her face. Big Tom seemed like he couldn't take it no more, excused himself to the men's room. Johnny was holding down Josephina with his right arm, trying to fork up his lettuce with his left and he ain't no lefty so lettuce ended on the white tablecloth. Tara reached over and tried to pull that little girl away, but she wasn't having it, clawed her grandma's bare arm. Scratches deep and red come close to drawing blood. Who'd have thought a four-year-old had the strength.

Big Tom come back, said he was going to have to go to his job. Him going moved me closer to Tara and I seen she was drunk off one glass of champagne. I give Johnny a look like we'd better pay and get out of here. He was getting some lettuce in his own mouth and forking some into Josephina's and Carlos was looking at them like he'd never seen the like. He'd ordered crab cakes that took a while coming.

Tara was getting started on another long story about Johnny when he was little and what a handful he was raising him as a single mom when would you believe it Tony Lafitte walked in carrying a big black bag. How he knowed where we was I never had a chance to ask but it wouldn't surprise me none if Johnny notified his father he was getting married. There being a spare place at the table Tony sat himself down without asking and Tara ruffled up like a wet hen, drew herself tight up against me like I was going to save her from some wild animal. She and Tony been divorced for years, you'd think the heat had kind of gone out of it.

Tony started studying the menu and that's when I knew this damned thing was going to go on forever and tried to wedge out over Tara's knees but she wouldn't let me. You know how it is when you're trapped someplace and have to make the best of it, so I made a rabbit out of my napkin for Josephina and that did keep her quiet for a while. No way I was going to eat that bloody hamburger.

Carlos was looking kind of ashy like he'd already had dealings with Tony Lafitte, who was said to have links with big-time mobsters in Chicago. He paid Carlos no more mind than if he was a fly, waved the waiter over ordered soup steak dessert. I started thinking we should of brought sleeping bags.

"I guess it's time for me to congratulate you," Tony said looking at his son. They was as alike as two pennies both shined up for the occasion and I guessed their black shoes under the table looked like four arrows.

"Well sure, Dad," Johnny said, cucumber cool, and Tony said "Congrats," not looking at Carlo,s then reached across for my champagne glass and stood up. Everybody in that place turned to look when he got started, having the kind of voice gets people's attention.

"Well I never thought to raise no pansy," he said, raising my glass that was still half full, "but that's what happened and I'm here to tell you all I'm fine with it. No grandkids but I got plenty from the others. Stand up here, Carlos, and let's us shake hands."

Carlos acted like he wanted to play dumb but no hope of that with Tony, so he stood up and reached and Tony shook his hand like he was going to shake it off. "Which one of you is the husband in this situation?" he asked.

"We don't go by that way of looking at it," Johnny said quick as a wink.

"That may be, son, but the world looks at it that way and so do I and seems to me this here Carlos is the husband."

Tara was wrestling loose of my arm fixing to rise up and go at him but Tony took one look at her and she fell back. "Looking good, Tara," he said. "Hard to believe you are seventy-four."

"Seventy-three same as you, Tony," she belted out, "and no easy life once you took off."

"Long time ago, you should of got over it, darlin'," he said. "Lord knows I have. Twenty-seven years, ain't it?"

"More like twenty-eight and every one of them a trial."

"Well you might of knowed what was coming the way this Johnny here carried on the day I left," he said smooth and modest. "Got a grip on my pants leg and wouldn't let go."

"It was not having money nearly took me down," Tara said. "Johnny got over missing you pretty quick."

Then it was quiet, nobody knowing what to say. The waiter come with them giant menus asking about dessert but nobody had the appetite except Tony who had asked for chocolate cake, sat there eating it fork by fork. When he was done and pushed the plate away Johnny called for the bill.

Tony reached down come up with his big black satchel unzipped it took out a black velvet-looking bag. Loosened the drawstring pulled out a silver pitcher with a top to it.

"My God that's a martini shaker," Tara said like she was scandalized. "Don't you know Johnny's AA?"

Tony Lafitte paid her no mind, passed the thing to Carlos, said, "Read what it says."

Carlos shifted it toward the light. "Carlos and Johnny, September 14, 2024," he read off in a tone like beside an open grave. "It's all about love."

"Well I don't know about that," Tara said in a grump voice and right then Tony Lafitte reached over and grabbed her and planted a big wet kiss on her cheek.

"But I do," he said.

HIS GRANDS

Cowboy's first grandchild, a boy named Marco, was black. That didn't come as any surprise to Cowboy. Marco's other side grandmother was some kind of Asian and the baby's father was black. So why not a black baby, shiny and beautiful! Cowboy dared anybody to disagree.

Cowboy himself was a breed and proud of it, holding up his handsome head in any gathering, Indian or Anglo. He'd married early, just out of the army and maybe spoiled—he said so himself—by the comfort women who operated just off the base in Okinawa. Those Asian girls asked for so little, a slice of pizza, a sandwich, a bottle of beer. Cheap perfume was a real treat, not like the whores at home in Oklahoma who demanded cash and plenty of it.

Cowboy, being only nineteen, fell in love with a not overused whore, Asian she said but black as the ace of spades. Took no precautions (being nineteen and in love) and married her when she turned up pregnant even though he had no way of knowing if it was his. The baby daughter turned out blacker than Cowboy had expected—his mixture didn't seem to figure—but that was the roll of the dice and she was beautiful! Her mom didn't want to leave Japan so when his tour was up, Cowboy took the baby—Mom was going back to the life—and went home.

He named this daughter Sheba after a queen he'd heard about but when his grandpa, Old Jake Bear, said no he changed it to Tammy and that went down better. Took her over to the Jesuit mission to be baptized and raised her riding beside him in his pickup.

Before she turned eighteen, Tammy run off and met up with this black boy who got her pregnant and their baby boy was black although a shade lighter than her mother, more Cowboy's kind of tan. That pleased him. He didn't go for the name Marco but let that pass.

He was glad when the black dude took off.

Cowboy had a special feeling for this grandson, watched him when his mother was working at Walmart, the dude having left her with nothing.

He took over when Marco was two and Tammy turned to drugs. Most nights Marco slept in bed with him till Tammy, just out of rehab and clear-minded for a day or two, called IHS and talked to the social worker and registered a complaint. Then Cowboy had to build Marco a sort of closet just big enough for his bed with a door that locked. The judge insisted on the lock for no reason Cowboy could see. He'd always respected the boy's privacy.

That same year Cowboy hitched up with a crazy white woman because he hadn't yet done his duty by the tribe. It was never said in words but all the men over fourteen knew they had to sire at least five live babies. That flock of babies would make up over time for their losses: war, disease, displacement. He didn't tell that to his new woman but when she started showing and fussed about being pregnant "with no ring" and talked about an abortion, he told her over his dead body.

"So you are a barbarian," she screeched and was out the door, good riddance. He tracked her down later and got the baby, another girl, named her Bonnie Blue. She was close to white and pretty as a picture though kind of wild later. By sixteen she'd gotten together with a Crow man married to somebody else and had three fast, boy, girl, boy, so Cowboy had made his minimum and could quit after one more shot with a cousin that didn't take.

But then Bonnie Blue started shouting they were her man's kids, not Cowboy's, and he had no right to claim them. He was paying for just about everything out of his subsidy and thought that maybe gave him the right but no. So he was still one short and knew he'd have to give it another try.

The crazy white woman come back, saying she forgave him though Cowboy didn't know what for but she was a proven breeder with five of her own so he bedded her a couple of times and sure enough it took. This time it was a boy as close to white as a baby could be and Cowboy, feeling too old to fight, let his mother take him off to the Cities and never saw either one of them again.

Cowboy turned seventy that summer and decided he was ready to retire from the baby-making business.

Now here come Marco, fourteen and a big boy, talking about how he wanted to celebrate Cowboy's seventieth birthday on July eleventh in the worst heat of the summer. Stood right by his recliner and went on till Cowboy told him in plain words he didn't see nothing to celebrate. "Knees not working so good, stomach don't tolerate whiskey, lady business over and done for—what you see for me to celebrate?"

"Living," that big boy said. "A lot of the mens around here never make it this far."

"You're right about that, even the clean-living ones get struck down sometimes, seems they go first."

"It's your seventieth and I aim to make you a pineapple upside down-cake."

"Where you learn to make cakes?"

"Working at the Bumblebee after school. That's their specialty. I watched Herman make it a couple of times."

"Herman that fancy man. I don't feature you hanging around with him."

"Don't worry, Cowboy, I like the girls just the way you used to."

"Well then you inherited something useful."

"So you going to let me?"

"Don't know how I can stop you."

And so it went. That big boy turned up crack of dawn on the eleventh, grocery bag full of stuff to make his cake. Cowboy's oven never had been used regular and he thought maybe it would fail but it went on and heated up while that boy was mixing eggs and other things. Had to go next door to borrow a eggbeater from Dorreen who was always cooking. Come back put everything together then no cake pan but Dorreen had that too. By now Cowboy was watching pretty close, admiring as he did anybody who could do something right and this boy could though it riled him to see a boy cooking. The world was changing he knew, though too late for him which was fine and maybe Marco would get a job at someplace making cakes.

While the cake was cooking they sat on the two chairs at the kitchen table waiting and here come Leroy. Cowboy guessed he was invited special by Marco without asking first. Leroy was coming off a five-day drunk and smelled like he always bought the cheapest wine he could find. Cowboy looked at Marco to show he was surprised and not in a good way but Marco never looked at him and then Leroy dug around in his pocket and pulled out a present wrapped in some sorry piece of silver paper. Handed it to Cowboy who took it and opened it there being no other way to go and it was a big toke and he thanked Leroy. Cowboy saw no reason to thank him it being the first time he'd seen Leroy since the fire nineteen years ago. He didn't appreciate the opportunity.

Marco pulled in another chair for Leroy and Leroy went and sat down like he was welcome.

The cake started to smell done and Marco took it out of the oven and sprinkled some sugar on it and went to cutting slices while it was still hot. Before he handed them around he sung "Happy Birthday" in a frail-sounding voice that was changing and Leroy had the nerve to join in and then went and slapped Cowboy on the shoulder.

"Happy birthday old man," he said in his voice that always sounded like it would have done better for a dog.

Cowboy pulled back. "Don't you old man me you son of a bitch." Would have punched him too but Marco got between them.

"Time to let all that go, it's so long ago," he said, and Cowboy felt his hand on his arm. Boy was stronger than he looked and Cowboy was not going to fight him. Always his favorite grandson, even now.

"Why'd you have to go and invite Leroy?" he said.

"Time for you to forget all that. You live ten yards apart, getting old together."

Cowboy didn't remember being young like Marco but it seemed to him he never had been that foolish.

"Now you two shake and I'll serve the cake," Marco said, and Cowboy saw the sweat gleaming on his black forehead.

He was not going to hold out his hand but Leroy reached over and grabbed it and shook it hard. "I didn't aim to make it tough for you," he said.

"You lied to that judge like a chicken heart saying I started the fire."

"Well in a way—"

"You fetched the gasoline can, splashed it on."

"Yeah but you lit it."

"Burnt that chapel to the ground," Marco said a kind of wonder in his voice. "Took the brothers five years to raise the money build it back."

"God damn it they learned their lesson! Worth five years in the pen," Cowboy said. "They respect us now, know we have our own religion."

"I'm handing out the cake," Marco said.

The three of them started to shovel it in. It was good and sweet and Cowboy ate it so fast he almost choked. Leroy and Marco was watching him, waiting for him to blow up again but he'd finished with that now and just wanted to eat his cake.

"I got a present for you too," Marco said when they had licked up the last crumb. He took a wrapped package out of his backpack and handed it to Cowboy, who just sat and stared at the paper with roses on it.

"Go ahead, open it," Leroy said.

Cowboy tore off the paper and there was a store-bought cardboard box. He took off the lid and pulled out a silver-looking frame with a picture in it. It took him a minute to figure out all the faces. Marco was in a hurry and named them all.

Cowboy's grands. Some tall, some short, some white, some brown, and one which was Marco black.

"I'll set it on your chifferobe," Marco said and put it there and then the three of them sat and looked at it.

"Ain't you proud?" Leroy asked him. "I don't have but the one."

"I ain't proud of anything that easy," Cowboy said.

"And all of them doing good like me," Marco said.

Cowboy didn't plan to dispute that, though working at that coffee place didn't count for good in his book and the others just as pitiful: nail lady, some kind of body work or fixing hair, minimum wage at best, no benefits, but he'd be long gone by the time they had to stop working because of age and needed to find somebody to help them get by.

Then like it wasn't already too much Marco struck up with "Happy Birthday" and Leroy with his voice like a rusty wheel running over rocks come in too.

Before Cowboy could stop him Marco kissed him on the cheek. “Happy birthday, Granddad.” Leroy would have done the same but Cowboy elbowed him off. “I need to lay down,” he said.

They shoved off then and Cowboy stretched out on the old sofa and pulled the blanket up to his chin and dreamed of the cheering at the rodeo when they give him his next silver buckle.

HOW THE WEST WAS WON

Cowboy had bought Jezebel cheap at auction because she had a deformed forelock. She was the best-tempered mare he'd ever owned. He usually went for geldings. She'd learned roping and cutting like she was born to it and for years Cowboy took her to rodeos, pulling his horse trailer with his old beat-up truck and soon had a drawer full of silver buckles to show for it.

Before long winning got too easy and he started to train Jezebel to dressage. It took a couple of years but then he started to win all the dressage events in that part of the West and up in Colorado and one summer in Canada but the fees was getting him down so he decided to retire after one more win at Colorado Springs and that's when he met Mona.

He didn't usually go to concerts not having much interest in that kind of crooning (bluegrass guitar was his thing) but he went that one time and ended up sitting next to her.

Mona. She was expensive, he saw that right off, out of his league, pearls and all, but she was plenty warm and friendly and asked him out after the music for a drink.

He'd quit drinking three years previous with the help of a certain program but he went with her to the next-door bar and after he explained Mona ordered him Perrier. He didn't want her to know he never had drunk that kind of water so he put down two full glasses and had to leave the table when he started belching. She was still warm and friendly when he come back and asked him up to her house in the foothills and it was the first house of that kind Cowboy had been in. The chandelier in the hall had about a thousand light bulbs on it and Mona didn't turn them off when they went upstairs.

Cowboy knew what was coming. It'd worked that way with all the white ladies he'd known. Mona called next day to ask him why he'd left in the middle of the night and he told her the usual, work, though he didn't have any work and it was getting serious. He owned his little house trailer parked for free on the side of a mountain road and the clothes he stood up in and his saddle and bridle and riding pants and spurs and a stall in a boarding barn for Jezebel. He'd planned to sell her when the price of hay and oats got too high but the first thing Mona did was give him money for a month's feed with more to come. He knew he'd never get a good price for the mare because of her deformed forelock though it never had held her back in the arena so he gave in knowing where it would lead.

Mona was no horsewoman. Tennis was it for her and Cowboy barely missed being roped into a game. He didn't plan on being humiliated that early on.

He liked her well enough—she was pretty good in bed though she yelled a lot to let him know she was coming—but he liked his freedom more so when she started to call every day at the crack of dawn he knew he was going to have to do something.

He didn't want to hurt her and besides there was the money so he answered her calls most of the time and saw her on Saturday nights and she was as satisfied as any of them could be and sang, "Clean white shirt on a Saturday night" as though that was all she wanted.

When she started to go on about buying a ranch he took it in stride and encouraged her. The cops had just run him off his roadside roost and he couldn't afford a trailer park even if he'd been willing to stay in one and so he had to find another way. And he knew ranching.

They spent two weeks off and on with a bandy-legged real estate agent visiting properties within fifty miles of town but Mona shied at the prices so they started looking further out. The agent took them to a bare mesa in the middle of nowhere with a barn and a cabin and the price was right and Mona bought it with cash. She said she wanted peace and quiet to meditate and write in her journal and look at the stars and she wanted Cowboy with her.

The mesa was dry desert and the wind whipped across it day and night. The only trees were stunted pinion and juniper and there was no grass because there was no water but the barn was in decent shape and Cowboy began to see the place had possibilities.

Then the Covid come and Cowboy wanted to move out of town.

One Saturday he picked up Mona in his truck to go out to the mesa.

"What's all that stuff in back?" she asked.

"Just some things I need."

"Are you planning on moving out to the ranch?"

He gave his head a little bow. "With your permission."

"You have my permission," she said, "but I'm coming too."

That didn't seem like much of a threat because by then he knew how she lived, off somewhere every few weeks with the habit of going what she called abroad for a month in the summer and friends and family all over the place she had to visit.

It worked pretty good that first Covid winter. Mona

drove out on Fridays smelling sweet and bringing a big box of supplies, always a steak, and Cowboy would build up the woodstove so she could fry that steak on top. He liked his well done and she learned to cut off a piece for herself that was next to raw and fry up the rest for him the way he liked it.

She helped him some with the chores but she never had worked and one time when he asked her to help him pick stones out of the dirt road—he liked things to look neat—she said she didn't aim to do stoop labor and went on in the cabin and that night she took the steak off the woodstove too soon. He couldn't eat it and left and went to Romeroville for steak tacos and when he got back she blew up at him and he saw it was no dice. Two things he couldn't stand, women yelling or crying and she did both so he moved back to town and bunked with a friend.

Some time passed and the Covid went away and that first spring free of it Mona come looking for him. She'd lost weight and looked her age which was well over sixty.

"I can't manage the ranch by myself," she said, standing on the other side of the screen door where he was bunking.

"Hire somebody," Cowboy said. He was still pretty sore.

"I want to hire you," she said.

He held off for a while thinking she was aiming to get him back in bed but she was offering good money so he said he'd try it for a month. He didn't move back in the cabin where they'd lived together but brought his house trailer up to the mesa a couple times a week, worked some and spent the night. Mona was almost never there.

The ranch wasn't good for raising anything but pinion, juniper, and weeds. He kept the weeds away from the cabin and put out salt blocks for the deer. Mona started saying it was a wildlife habitat. Then he put out corn for the wild turkey and here they come, an army of them led by a big old cock fierce and bright as a falling star and Mona was pleased and said they should put the ranch in easements so it could never be developed. Cowboy knew it was never going to be developed unless for a wind farm but he liked her being pleased and stayed quiet. And it was done. That was when she told him she was leaving the ranch to him in her will and he let her believe he believed her.

He knew that she wanted more though she knew better than to say it—he could tell from the way she stood too close to him whenever he gave her the chance.

One spring night at the ranch she went to pawing at him and he told her to stop.

"I don't know why you're shouting at me," she said. "You used to like it."

"A while ago."

"I've kept my looks, I'm in good shape, work hard

on it," she said and even lifted up her shirt to show him her abs, pretty good for an old woman. "Why don't you want me?"

She had tears in her eyes but she didn't let them run because Cowboy couldn't stand tears.

"You can't have a baby," he said.

"You told me you've made enough." She was sobbing and he knew he had to get out of there fast.

"Still the only reason to do it far as I know," he said, reaching for his hat and heading for the door.

"Well then I'm going to sell the ranch," she sobbed, and he stopped. He didn't care one way or the other—he had his house trailer and a lady rancher had told him he could park it on her spread—but it cut him that this was the only way Mona with all she had thought she could hurt him.

"That's pitiful," he said.

Then he left her sobbing and begging and he knew it was not the end of it, there never was going to be an end because he'd started feeling sorry for her.

Well it took a while but they worked out a way they could both stand. Mona was going to spend one Sunday a month at the ranch "seeing how things are going" like he was just a ranch hand which was what he wanted or thought he did. "And do spend the night when you're out there working if you feel like it but please please don't bring some woman to sleep in our bed."

He felt no need to tell her he'd retired from that occupation.

It was working pretty good till Old Man Thundercloud had to stick his nose in, those tribal people never let family go.

"Bring that woman up here for Pickle's death party," he said. Pickle was some kind of cousin who'd killed himself with a whiskey bottle.

Cowboy worked up and down the excuses but Thundercloud was stubborn as they come and wouldn't take any of them and Cowboy knew if he didn't bring Mona it'd dig a hole in all his relations. "You ashamed of us or what?"

It just about killed him to see how pleased Mona was, like a kid with a bag of candy. She wanted him to help her chose an outfit for the giveaway but he just told her to wear something decent. Old as she was she sometimes put on those short skirts.

They started out on Friday, drove all night with Mona snoozing and got to the rez late the next afternoon, sun setting behind the mountains.

She didn't say nothing when she saw the way they lived but he could hear the words shoved down in her throat and felt sorry for her, so keen to please him she'd strangle herself with words she knew he'd hate. She had no way of knowing he'd thought those same words so many times he was kind of numb to them.

The give-away was about to start and she seemed surprised by the size of the table and all the goods laid out on it: canned hams, whiskey, beer, sodapop, cigarettes, even a old saddle. "Did all this belong to Pickle?" she asked and of course the answer was no. It was given by friends and family to honor the dead.

No snatching or grabbing but a slow procession around the table and hands reaching out for this or that. They needed everything bad but never let it show.

Cowboy took one of the hams and let it go at that. Thundercloud was watching him and Cowboy took his lady over and introduced her to him and to Aunt Your Mean Horse he hadn't seen in years. She looked old and gray but he remembered how kind she'd been to him when he was young and gave her a smack-kiss on the cheek and she wrinkled up with smiles.

"Come here, Jessie, and meet your uncle," she called to a big girl around fifteen years old who was swallowing a bag of chips. She came over like it was a pain and Cowboy remembered she was the girl the state took from her mother years before because the house was such a mess.

The girl didn't stay for more than a minute and from the look of her, Cowboy knew why Aunt Your Mean Horse had gotten so old and gray. He knew a wild filly when he saw one.

"You raising her?" he asked.

"Trying but I can't do nothing with her. She outgrowed her foster family, come back here, her mom has to work and sent her over to me. What was I going to say. But I'm old, Cowboy, and she's likely to send me to my grave before my time, out all night and so on, you know the kind."

"Takes a firm hand on the reins," Cowboy said. Mona was nodding.

"Just look at my hands, no strength left in them," Auntie said, holding out two spotted and speckled specimens limp as weeds cut and left in the sun. "I need help, Cowboy."

"You want me to take her?" he asked.

Mona said quiet, "I expect we could do it, Cowboy." First thing she'd ever said that surprised him.

Auntie heard it and her face lit up. "Would you do it? She's registered, gets her subsidy regular, wouldn't cost you much."

Just cost me my life, Cowboy thought.

Auntie called Jessie over and she come wiping salt from the chips off her chin. "You lucky girl, your uncle's going to take you for a visit, get you out of here like you're always asking," Auntie said.

Jessie looked at Cowboy. "Do I got to go to school?"

"Sure do," he said and Mona put in that they had a real nice school just a few miles from the ranch and Cowboy felt the plan closing around him before he'd decided for sure.

Aunt Your Mean Horse got Jessie's clothes packed up in no time, scared Cowboy was going to change his mind. Jessie started to get in the truck shotgun but Cowboy told her that was Mona's seat and she made a face but slid on in the back.

They drove out, hit the highway. Cowboy started telling her about his rules but stopped when Mona touched his hand. "That'll come later," she said and craned back over the seat to ask Jessie what shows she liked to watch and which bands she enjoyed and the girl acted like nobody hadn't ever asked her those things before.

Cowboy knew what was happening but let it roll over him like a wave with Mona chattering and laughing and the girl doing the same. "I expect we can make this work if you give it a chance" was all he found to say and neither one of the females took much notice.

It got tougher after they got back and Mona left for her house in town and Cowboy had to lay out the rules: school every day and that meant up at six to fix her own breakfast and ready for him to ride her there at seven-thirty sharp, no going out on school nights and ten p.m. curfew on the weekends. Jessie didn't like any of that but it seemed like she knew she was going to have to listen to him and Mona would be there from time to time to make the medicine go down smoother.

So they got through the spring but then summer come and no school and Jessie passed her sixteenth birthday, took Cowboy's truck one night and stayed out till dawn.

He was waiting for her when she come back jingling his keys in her hand looking like she'd growed an inch and gained ten pounds where it counted overnight.

"You're grounded for a month," he told her, thinking where could he hide his keys then knew he'd have to sleep with them under his pillow.

"Oh Uncle," she said like he was being foolish, and he wished for Mona who would have smoothed it out somehow. "I've heard a lot about how you like to party."

"Not no more," he said, "and you neither till you graduate and get your first job."

"Oh Uncle," she said again in that pussy-cat voice and sidled up to him and went to give him a kiss.

"Cut that out," Cowboy said, blocking her with his arm. She was a big girl and he could feel the heat rising off her.

"I know you like me," she said. "I seen you looking at me."

"I like you when you behave," he said wishing strong for Mona.

She brushed up against his arm and he felt the edge of her big boobs pushing through her shirt and that other smell meant some guy had been in her.

"I think you're mighty handsome, Uncle," she said.

He swatted her then to make her back off and when

she started to cry he told her, "Don't you ever try to pull your tricks on me again. You're my niece and I aim to raise you decent."

"You're mean," she said, sobbing a little, but she backed off and Cowboy knew it was just the first round but he'd won it.

That night he called Mona which he never did, closed up in the closet so Jessie wouldn't hear. "I can't hardly do anything with her," he said and told the whole story.

After a minute Mona said, "You want me to come out there and help you?"

"Well I know that would seem like a hardship—"

"Do you need me?" she asked, interrupting him before he could finish.

The yes he strangled out was the toughest word he'd ever spoken.

He heard her little soft laugh on the other end of the line and thought if she moved in with him he might kill her.

Mona came out started in right away with a long talk with Jessie, sitting on the side of the bed before the girl was hardly even awake. She'd closed the door so Cowboy couldn't hear a word which pissed him off because he felt like he could have come up with a few clues but all he knew was the talk went on a long time and then Mona came out and made two cups of some kind of herbal tea, took the cups in to Jessie and never offered Cowboy anything.

He went out to feed Jezebel and kicked the stall door three times hard when it wouldn't open. Went back in the cabin and they was still twittering away in there with the door closed and he went out and threw the saddle on Jezebel and whipped her and rode her to sweating, all the way to the end of the mesa.

He drew up there, the mare panting and trembling. Sun rising in the eastern sky when he looked down over the bluff and saw the shadows already gathering in the deep valley. He wondered how many years he had left and reached down and patted Jezebel's neck and turned her and rode back at a slow trot. He thought of the drawer full of silver buckles and who in the world would want them and got back to the cabin and washed Jezebel down with water from the hose and went back to the house.

Mona was cooking something on the stove and Jessie was sitting at the kitchen table. She had put on clothes.

"I fixed us something special," Mona said. "It's called ratatouille but it's really just eggplant and tomatoes," and she picked up a clean spoon and dipped some. "Here, try it."

And Cowboy did.

TAKING CARE

Maybe I had no business calling Uncle Cowboy. That's what Mom'd say when she come home from work but the baby was spitting up all over, shit coming out the other end too. And did he stink. Fast as I got him cleaned up it started all over till I give him a swat just a little one and then the howling.

IHS is a hour drive. Don't know what docs could do anyhow 'bout the mess coming out both ends of him 'less plug him up somehow.

Driving's no problem. I been driving since I turned eight but Mom said she'd whup me if I took the baby somewhere in Great-Grandpa Jake Bear's old red Ford truck so I called Unc.

He started in right away. "Why ain't you in school?"

"Mom has to work to keep Section Eight so this is my job."

"My God and you nine years old."

"Ten last July."

"What in hell you do with him?"

"He stops puking and shitting I aim to get him going on the video game. So far he ain't interested just bangs the keys and laughs."

"What about Great-Grandma Blacksleeves?"

"She told Mom she already put in her time with babies. She's at the casino mainly."

"Well you know I can't come up there. Rodeo's Saturday."

I didn't know.

"Anyway I don't know nothing about babies."

"You made six of 'em," I said.

"Mainly their moms raised them. That him I hear screaming?"

"Nobody else."

"Well put something in his mouth, candy or something."

"Nothing like that around here," I said.

"No use trying to talk in this commotion." Unc hung up.

I don't blame him much. He rides the rodeo circuit, wins them silver first place buckles, comes home to a pretty white lady, food on the table, plenty of beer.

Next thing I knowed somebody banging on the door. I looked out the window, seen this white van with the state's sun sign. Government.

She shouted through the door, "May I come in?"

I never know why they so goddamn polite. They know they can come in anytime and we can't say nothing.

"Baby cutting up is all," I told her through the door like that'd run her off.

"Your uncle called said you alone here."

I turned the key, she come on in.

She got started the way I knowed she would, how I ought to be in school. I told her the only way we have this place is if Mom works.

"This crazy system," she said. She went to looking round the room with her clipboard, writing down what's wrong. Dirty dishes in the sink, diapers soaking in the toilet. She was a nice sight, bright red nails, lipstick to match, blue skirt stuck to her like paint.

She finished writing, said, "I got to make a report."

"How come?" I said.

"It's against the law, little boy left home alone to care for a infant."

I told her, "I ain't no little boy, be eleven next July, he way too big to be a infant."

"Anyway you look at it it's wrong," she said looking at the baby sleeping on the couch like she wanted to eat him. "You'll be hearing from us."

She went out to the van and drove off. I knowed what was coming. State already took Jessie last year,

Mom screaming she's going to clean up the house didn't make no difference.

Well Unc started it but it was up to me to end it. I packed diapers and four filled bottles and some wipes in a garbage bag, wrote a note to Mom left on the kitchen table, piled the baby in his stroller thank God still sleeping and rolled him out of there. Had to go back for a couple of mouth stoppers for when he woke up and started screaming. Seemed like he'd gotten in the habit.

We rolled on down the dirt road, stroller wheels hitching on stones. No use going to cousins', State'd look there first. Cold, snow coming on. I figured Old Jake Bear's barn full of holes, years since he died and quit tending to it. So no use.

I got us out on the highway but no good staying there, eyes in all the cars. Baby woke up, looked around, got interested and didn't go to screaming. I figured a lot of his screaming is 'cause he's bored, closed up in that hencoop house with me. His dad don't come by regular, when he does more than not he's drunk looking for a handout. Not my dad, he's been gone awhile in the pen.

Traffic roaring by I had to get us off that highway fast. I turned the first road, I come to casino, snow falling hard I put the garbage bag over him but he don't care for that, commenced squalling. I stuck one of the mouth stoppers in, he went to sucking and shut up.

Our casino's big all kinds of ways in, porches and all. I drove us in under one of the porches, pushed the stroller through the big door. Security lady standing there yawning said, "No kids allowed." Back of her machines clicking blinking.

"We out in a snowstorm," I said. It was coming down hard. "Please let me keep him in here a while."

She looked at the baby, bare legs and feet red with cold, said, "Well for a few minutes while I go check with somebody."

She went off. I knew what'd happen if I stayed so I rolled us on through the machines. Great-Aunt Your Mean Horse at one of them, too busy pulling levers to look around.

Door at the back to some kind of little room full of junk. I rolled us on in. No window nor nothing. I didn't put on the light, might show under the door. It was eat time. I pulled a filled bottle out the garbage bag and tried to warm it under my arm. Didn't do much so I pulled out the mouth stopper and stuck the nipple in. Baby made some kind of terrible face, I just pushed the nipple in and went to rubbing his throat like I seen men do with orphan lambs they bottle raising. Baby commenced to sucking. Milk went down fast cold or not. I burped him on my shoulder laid him back in the stroller, pushed the mouth stopper in quick. He was back to sleep pretty fast.

I laid down on a pile of old pillows smelled like dried puke, took me a little nap. Mom'd be home now worrying but wasn't nothing I could do. She had my note.

We stayed there all that night, nobody come bothering us. Baby slept pretty good, up early for another bottle. I seen I only had two left. Changed him, hid his dirty diaper in the corner behind some broke chairs. It was warm in that room. We both went back to sleep.

I knowed it was opening time when I heard cleaners talking outside our door and the early birds coming in. Had a piece of jerky in my pocket, chewed on that. Changed the baby again, give him another bottle. Only one left.

Door opened, in come Unc. How'd he know? No use asking, he don't take to questions. Said, "Get your stuff, let's go."

"All I got's in this garbage bag. We need milk."

"OK, get going."

We flew out of there. Great-Aunt Your Mean Horse been there all night, never looked around.

Unc's truck parked near the door, we went right to it. He jumped the stroller in the back. I grabbed the baby, got in shotgun I thought, but Jose sitting there. I went in the back seat, got the baby settled pretty comfortable, said to Unc, "Where to?"

"You are not going back to that shack," he said, pulling out of the parking lot.

"Mom'll be crying."

"Cry as much as she likes, it don't change the situation. You coming home with me."

I wanted to say the white lady going to like that? But Unc don't answer questions.

We was passing Family Dollar. "We need milk."

"WE don't need milk," Unc said, he particular that way, got educated all the way up at the Jesuits'.

"Baby does," I said, "'less you want to hear screaming."

"OK." He pulled in, got out, run in, way up in years but still running like a kid.

Jose turned around. "How come you got stuck with the kid?"

"Mom has to work." I was getting sick of telling everybody.

"They's such a thing as babysitters."

"She don't have the cash. Grandma dead, Great-Grandma's wore out, can't do no more."

"Well if you think your uncle has the patience to put up with that thing screaming night and day..."

I said, "We got to take the chance."

Jose shook his head. He's been in the picture a long time, plaster work on houses Unc is building, knows the situation pretty well.

Unc come running back with a paper bag, pushed it over the seat at me. "He need it now?"

"Not yet, he's still sleeping. I need to warm it."

"Once we get to my place," Unc said, pulling out.

"What you going to do about the rodeo?"

"That's tomorrow."

We went on to Jose's house on the south side of town. Jose got out, wished us luck.

"We going to need it," Unc said.

"What your lady going to say?" Jose asked through the window.

"My house, she don't have no say."

Another half hour we got there, fine-looking place a little ways out of town. Unc got out, went in. I took my time getting the baby in the stroller. He woke up, looked around, got interested, didn't go to screaming.

Unc was at the front door when we rolled up, white lady just behind him. "Come in to your new home," she said over his shoulder.

"Mom's goin' to want us back," I said.

Unc said, "She may want but she's not fit. If I have to I'll go to court to prove it.

I rolled the stroller in. Great big hall with a ceiling higher than trees and the mountains through the big windows. How Unc has the money I don't know. He works construction pretty regular with Jose but that don't pay for any mansion. I guess the white lady owns it.

She all smiles, pink face, round cheeks, lips painted. "Come on to your new room."

I followed her, rolling down a hall long as a bowling

alley. She opened a door, lets me in. Nice bed, chest of drawers, the whole enchilada. "This room's for you. I'll put the baby next door."

"He needs to be with me, I feed him."

She looks like she's going to dispute me but Unc's right in back of her. "I'll get that old crib," he says.

He comes back with this antique. Spokes in the sides busted but the mattress looks pretty clean. "Lay him in here," he says. "Who's his daddy?"

I lay him down, he goes to staring round but stays quiet.

"Mom's new man, that David. He's mostly gone."

"Your mom sure knows how to pick 'em, like your dad wasn't bad enough."

I don't aim to go that way. Truth is Unc was the same way, drunk and fighting till he made whatever money he made however he made it and built some of them mansions for the Texas people. Looks like that satisfied him and now he has the lady.

She says, "I'll warm the milk," wanting to get in some way.

I hand her the last bottle. "Just a little warm, not hot." Unc goes with her.

I sit down on a thick chair so good to feel I put my head back and doze for about a minute.

Lady come back with Unc, hands me the bottle. I squirt a drop on the inside of my wrist the way I seen

Mom do. Warmed just so. I prop the bottle on the side of the crib, push the nipple in his mouth.

"Let me hold him," Lady says. Way she picks him up shows me she knows babies. Settles him in the crook of her right arm. He's still sucking, looks up at her with his big eyes. "I raised two of them," she says.

"Both graduated college," Unc says, watching her like a hawk. I suspicion he don't want her to have a whole lot to do with the baby but who else? I sure don't know how to hold him the way she does like it's natural. Mom always props the bottle.

Unc goes to the rodeo next day same as usual, wants me to come along and help but I tell him I need to stay with the baby till he's settled. Unc comes home late with a big silver buckle, first place in cutting, showed me a drawerful. Must have fifty buckles in there, all silver shining, says, "They don't want me to ride no more, say I'm too good."

"Good is what wins," I say.

"Want me to move aside for the younger ones."

"You going to do it?"

"Hell no," he says, slamming the drawer. "Once I train you, maybe."

I don't see no future in that. Last thing I'd tell Unc but I'm scared of horses ever since that one of his kicked me in the leg, nearly broke it for no reason.

We settle in, stay in the mansion all winter. Spring

come, Mom goes to court to get us back, claims to the judge her sister in Denver going to come live with us so I can get to school. Unc kicks up a fuss, his lady crying, but what can they do? Court ordered I'll have to go back home and start in at school.

If it was up to me I'd stay in the mansion, give the baby his bottle even if I don't know how to hold him in the crook of my arm. I'm his first friend and he knows me from anybody. It was me saved him from the State with a little help from Unc and I swear the baby knows it.

MR. JACOB

Hot. Cowboy was sitting on the porch of the government house he moved into when he turned eighty and headed back up to the rez where there was still some people might help him die when the time come. This porch had a concrete floor heated like a griddle with one spindly tree for shade so Cowboy was holding his red umbrella open over his head to keep off the sun. He was expecting the truck some time that morning and had a full cup of coffee balanced on his knee when Sam-the-Man, Bonnie Blue's youngest, walked up the three steps from the dirt and sat down on the other chair like he planned on staying.

"How come you letting Jake Bear's covered wagon go?" he said, fresh like they all was now.

"Jake Bear's been gone a long time, no use for that thing. I never did know why he bought it. Saw it in some junkyard somewhere, said he felt like he had to have it."

"Well but it's a antique, you could've sold it for a lot of money," Sam-the-Man said.

"Some things you don't sell," Cowboy told him, sipping his coffee. "It'll be took good care of in that museum in Taos and maybe sometime you'll drive me down there to visit it." Cowboy knew that was unlikely but in old age he'd sweetened a little, not enough to gripe him but enough to make everything he said go down easier.

"Well I don't like it," Sam-the-Man said. "Nothing left of the old days. I call that our history."

Cowboy let it go. It'd been left up to him to clear everything out when the ranch was sold, not a single one of these sorry-ass kids would help and the mess of old bridles, broke-back saddles, worn-out boots, and horse regalia went to the landfill along with the tables, beds, and chairs. Too much work to find folks to buy, probably wouldn't pay nothing for them anyway.

He looked Sam square in the face to shut him up. He was a scruffy kid, too fair to take the sun good, like his mother Bonnie Blue, red as a cherry throat lozenge by September. Sam should have gone off and enlisted if he'd had the sense to do what Cowboy told him but then Bonnie come whining about him getting killed over there in Iran and wasn't it enough she'd already lost his brother, that big bunch of foolishness called Grayhouse (what a name!). Cowboy didn't tell her what he knew, that big fat boy didn't understand nothing about taking care of himself and probably walked right into that sniper's sights. Anyway Bonnie Blue should've taken some comfort from the funeral the army give him with the Taps and the flag folded in a tight triangle and put in her arms. Cowboy's Uncle Tom that died in Vietnam never did get brung back for any funeral. Army said they lost track of him. But Bonnie Blue was that kind of woman never does take comfort.

Cowboy's arm was shaking from holding the red umbrella up so long and Sam leaned over, took it without asking first, folded it up. Cowboy didn't say nothing. Another thing to let pass but he put his eyes on Sam, looking. Watch out, boy.

Sam shut up under the weight of Cowboy's eyes and they sat there in the silence that was not friendly but was the way things went these days. Cowboy had let that rile him a little. Sam-the-Man was actually married to that big-boob girl from Sheridan, too young to do such a thing but there it was. More than a year, closer to two, and no babies.

"How come no babies?" Cowboy said, still nailing Sam with his eyes.

"She won't do it, Grandpa," Sam said, taking his eyes away and looking at the spindly tree. "Said I'd have to be making a million dollars a year."

"Well you'll never do that," Cowboy said, already a little more riled, "and she knows it."

"Good-paying jobs down on the rigs in the Permian but she won't put up with me going, says she knows what goes on in them man camps, whores and all."

"Lots of things worse than whores," Cowboy said, reaching way back in time to Okinawa. "That's what they called my first wife. It don't mean nothing, good-hearted woman is all."

"How come you never did marry any of the rest of them?" Sam asked which didn't relieve Cowboy of being riled.

"Not worth the fuss and bother," Cowboy said, going on before Sam could talk back. "You let that girl get the upper hand, Sam. Jake Bear used to say to any of us getting hitched, 'First thing you knock her down and stomp on her, then you won't have no more trouble.'"

"They don't stand for that these days," Sam said. "Jo Ann wouldn't drop her drawers for me till I said I'd marry her."

"Why you had to go and have that fancy wedding, bride dress and all, I hate to think what it cost you."

"She paid for everything, Grandpa. You know she's got that good job at the hospital."

"Watch out all that money don't plow you under," Cowboy said. "Maybe that's why you ain't made no babies."

Sam flushed up and was about to say something would have riled Cowboy more for sure, leading to words between them and maybe worse but here come Big

Boobs herself flying down the road in that new fancy red hybrid Cowboy knowed the price of. “Here she comes,” he said, sounding pleased in spite of himself. Since Milly died he’d been short of women.

She hopped out in her white nursey uniform, white stockings, shoes, the whole burrito, snatched that little white cap off her head, hair pouring down, trundled herself up the stairs, a big woman everywhere that counted.

“Hello, Grandpa!” she shouted and come right over and kissed him in the middle of his left cheek. She had that woman smell under the soap and the deodorant.

“I ain’t your grandpa,” Cowboy said, reaching up with his finger to feel where she’d kissed him.

“Sorry. I meant to call you Cowboy,” she said. “Hello, darlin’.” That was for Sam.

“Not that neither,” Cowboy said. It come to him just then. “I ain’t been near a horse in twenty-seven months. Knees won’t stand for it.”

She was grinning like she took him for an idiot, buttons on the front of her uniform stressed to busting. “What you want us to call you?”

“Jacob,” he said. “That’s my birth name and don’t never call me Jake. That name belongs to Jake Bear. Dead but it’s still his name.”

“All right, Mr. Jacob,” she said. He looked to see if she was laughing at him but she wasn’t.

Sam was taking it all in like it was food and drink. "You get some time off?" he asked her.

"A hour for lunch so I thought I'd drive out here, see how you two are doing." She dragged the old boot-taking-off stool over and sat down near Jacob's left knee. Oh she was a charmer all right, and he suspicioned her about as much as he enjoyed her, too long since he'd snuffed up that woman smell.

She asked him, "You getting hungry? Anything in the fridge I can heat up?"

"I don't want nothing. I'm waiting for that truck."

"You can eat and wait at the same time," she said and again he looked to see if she was laughing at him but she wasn't.

"Chili left over from last night," he said. It grieved Cowboy to see Sam go inside to heat it up.

Boobs pulled the stool closer and he got another whiff of her smell and knew he was going to have a time holding on to himself.

"You and me are due a talk," she said, taking a pack of cigarettes out of her pocket. "You want one?"

Cowboy reached for one. Doctor down at Indian Health would have a fit but so what.

She had matches and he put the cigarette in his mouth and she lighted it like she'd done it for him a hundred times and he drew in that first sweet dose. "So what the hell, fifty years of smokes ruint my lungs, it was worth it, you ask me."

"I know what you mean. Been a while since you got one in your mouth?"

"Sam went and threw out my last carton."

"I'll bring you some more," she said. They heard Sam slamming pots in the kitchen. "It'll take him a while to figure out how to warm up that chili," she said.

"So what you want to talk about?" Jacob asked, making a string of smoke rings so she'd squeal.

She didn't. "Sam says you're after him for us to have a baby."

"Isn't any 'us' about it," Jacob told her. "It's your job from the get-go."

"Not the way we look at it."

"That why you won't do it?"

A frown curled her face and he saw what she'd look like when she was old and was glad he wouldn't live to see it. She was too ripe, like one of them red and gold Indian peaches that bruise brown as soon as you touch them.

"I'm about to get a really great promotion at the hospital and a raise to go along with it. I'll be working longer hours, no time off for a baby. We need that promotion, Mr. Jacob."

He saw she'd settled into his name and was glad she was the first one to use it. "That's just money. You can't stack that up against making a baby, could be a boy."

"Well you know Sam didn't get that job patching roads for the tribal government."

"I wanted to put in a word for him, you wouldn't let me."

"Sam has to stand on his own feet now," she said, sounding as old and worn out as a regular rez woman. "That's part of our wedding contract."

"You got all that writ down on paper?"

"Yes, signed and dated. I don't go into anything blind."

Sam come out balancing three soup bowls on the crook of his arm and the chili smell made Jacob hungry. Half the time he didn't bother with heating up food, just stood in the cold air from the refrigerator and ate anything he saw laying on the shelves.

"Spoons," Boobs said, and Sam run to the kitchen to fetch them.

He come back and handed out three spoons and they all started shoveling. Chili wasn't real hot but in that weather so what. Maybe Sam didn't want to leave them together too long.

Well she had him under her thumb for sure and Jacob just hoped there was a payoff in bed.

Food made him tired these days and he threw a big yawn.

Boobs took his empty bowl and spoon. "You want to go and lay down?" she asked him all sweet.

"Honey draws them tiny ants, crawled right up under

the lid of my jar, drowned theyselves, I had to throw the whole mess out."

"You like vinegar better?" Jacob knew better than answer. Maybe Sam was under her thumb but he didn't plan to join the boy there.

" Go on and lay down. I'll watch for the truck," Sam said. "Wagon right there beside the road, shouldn't be no problem to load it."

Boobs was helping Cowboy up out of his chair before he said anything about needing help, and steering him on in the house. "Good to lay down for a while in this heat," she said like she was back to nursing.

Well once in a blue moon it wasn't going to do him no harm.

Inside his bedroom it was dark as the pit—he kept the shades down to keep out the heat—and she flipped on the lightbulb in the ceiling.

"My word, look at that," she said, letting go of him to go over to the chifforobe where he had his buckles laid out.

"I was shining them up, forgot to put them back in the drawer," he said. She was pawing them over, asking, "What's this one? What's that one?"

He told her the names of all those towns and cities where he'd rodeoed for fifty years: Deadwood, Silverton, Durango, San Antonio, Cody, Jackson, Denver, Albuquerque, Houston, Dallas, one time all the way to

California. Saying those names give him a ripple of that good feeling. He didn't tell her he got so expert before the end they started begging him to quit and let some of the young ones come up.

"Good money sometimes," he said, because they all thought that was the reason he kept on till his knees give out. "When I'm gone you and Sam take these buckles, get the silver melted down, pick out the turquoise, see what you can get, don't stop with the first offer."

She looked at him. "We'd never do that. These are history, Mr. Jacob."

"History's a dime a dozen," he said. "Just a lot of sweat and work and driving all night with the trailer seesawing and toward the end diesel prices so high. You melt them down, buy you something special."

She shook her head, watching him push the buckles into the chifforobe drawer and shut it. "Long time since I let anybody see them. Milly was the last."

"You miss her?"

"Well, she just give up on me with the diabetes. Never walked after they took her leg, wouldn't even try that leg I bought her with good money." It was standing in the corner, leaning against the wall.

"I thought those red shoes I bought her might help."

"Just turned her head to the wall when I tried to show them to her. I did put one on that leg."

They looked at the leg, straps dangling, the red shoe

still waiting to be walked in.

"I expect you're lonely," she said.

"Well no," he said. The last thing he wanted was her sympathy.

They heard Sam shout from the porch. "Here come the truck!"

He put off her helping hand and went out to the porch under his own steam and here come the eighteen-wheeler plowing up the dirt road, so wide it knocked down branches off the trees on both sides. Come up next to the wagon and stopped with the air brakes huffing and a guy in a baseball hat got out and come to the porch steps.

"You the folks want me to haul that old piece of shit down to the museum in Taos?"

Sam said, "That's a piece of history, mister. One of the last. You only seen the like in the movies."

"Whatever. I need to load it up and get going."

Jacob watched Sam go down to tell the man what to do. They had to hitch up the old mare, Star, the last horse Mr. Jacob had left, to the wagon and then she wouldn't pull. Sam went to find a whip but Mr. Jacob shouted, "I'll get her to move," and with Boobs's hand under his arm he went down the steps and walked up to his old horse. He said a few words into her sad old floppy ear and she leaned into the harness and got the wagon moving. The guy let down the tailgate and Mr. Jacob eased Star past those big wooden wagon wheels crusted with dirt from some long-ago time and up the ramp smooth as butter and with him beside her she dragged the wagon into the eighteen-wheeler and stood still and quiet till he got her unharnessed.

Soon as he turned the mare around and led her out of the truck the guy closed the tailgate.

"Ain't you going to fasten that wagon down?" Mr. Jacob asked.

"Nothing's going to hurt it between here and Taos," the guy told him and then he hopped up in his cab and backed that truck all the way out to the main road, breaking branches again along the way. The three of them just stood there staring.

"He'll knock that wagon to sticks the way he's going," Sam said.

"One way or the other that's the end of it," Jacob said, taking hold of Star's reins to start her to the barn. He got her in her stall with a dipper full of oats and went back to the porch hoping Boobs would put her hand under his elbow to help him up the steps which she did.

A week later some lady called him from the museum. "We're pleased to have your covered wagon," she said. "I'll send you the appraisal for your tax deduction later this week."

"I don't fool with taxes," Mr. Jacob said.

"I'm still going to send you the paperwork," she said, "in case you change your mind."

"Well all right."

"We're going to clean up your wagon and put it in our Ranch Days show next August. Maybe you'll find a way to come down."

"I don't drive no more," Mr. Jacob said.

"Isn't there somebody in your family?"

"Well I got a grown grandson or maybe his wife. She's got one of them new hybrids."

"Ask her to bring you—everybody here wants to meet you. Not too many of the old-timers left."

"I'll ask her," he said and knew as sure as morning Jo Ann would do it, new job or no new job, and Sam would stay home and between the two of them, they'd have a grand time.

COWBOY ALONE

After Mama Blacksleeves went and died on me, healthy as a horse one day then just dropped down the next, I was in a bad way. Turned out she left her Old Colorado Mining Stock to that sister in California she was always fussing about. Well I didn't expect much in that way from her though it would have come in handy but I also didn't expect her dying so early. Sister wanted her shipped to California for burying. I said alright. Cost a pretty penny.

Soon as the news got out IHS was after me. Said I was too old to live alone, claimed I was "frail," wanted to cart me off to the old folks' home. I was down there one time visiting Uncle Joe, him in a wheelchair in front of the TV had peed his pants didn't even know it. I got him to the bathroom, stripped him, him trying to hide himself with his hands like I was going to get a shock out of his old withered pizzle made a drove of kids in its day. Not a shock for me, I've seen a-plenty.

"I'll die before I'll go to that place," I told the IHS lady.

"Then we'll send somebody regular to check on you." She was standing in my door, holding the broke screen open. I didn't ask her in. Nice-looking but bent on trouble, I know the kind.

"What's he going to check?" I asked her.

"She. Food in the refrigerator, general hygiene, count your pills, make sure you're taking them."

I don't have no trouble flushing pills down the toilet, never did see they did me any good. Supposed to bring my pressure down. My pressure's part of me, always has been, never did me no harm. Might be the reason I'm still going strong, blood running around so fast.

Here the checker come the next day rattling the broke screen door when I didn't get to it quick enough. Ramona. Fat as a little hen and about that high. She come pushing in before I agreed to it, went round my room passing her finger over all surfaces. I don't claim to do much cleaning, Mama Blacksleeves took care of that kind of thing. Just one room, kitchenette, bath in these new apartments they put up on the edge of town. Government money means nothing's done right but Mama didn't care when the door come loose or linoleum in the kitchenette curled up. I don't pay it no mind. Life's too short for fussing.

This Ramona had her clipboard like they all do started in writing down everything needed fixing. "We'll have you shipshape in no time."

"I like things the way they are," I told her.

"We can't have you going downhill now your wife's passed."

"Mama Blacksleeves never did that much around here, always running off to the casino."

"Never speak ill of the dead," she said, stiff as a schoolteacher. "I'll send Roberto round tomorrow screw that screen door back on."

I didn't say nothing seeing she was set. I been on my own seven months now, kids dropping by every couple of weeks and Jason Looseleg now and then with a bottle and a pack of cards but most evenings it's me and the TV which is fine by me. I'd just as soon nod off to that racket, wrapped up warm in my chair, wake up when the moon sets or later.

I knowed right off this Ramona better not see me asleep in my chair, she'd find some way to put me in the home, claim I'm "incontinent." I have my blankets folded, TV off, whenever she come which takes some doing soon as I hear her car coming up the road.

Next day come this Roberto and I tell you he's a card. Has this nice little tool belt with a wrench and a hammer in it, his cap turned front to back two tails of black hair long as his arms.

"What can I do for you, Grandpa?" he says at me through the screen.

"Not a thing in this world, young man," I tell him.

"Ramona says this door is falling off its hinges." He gives it a shake. "I'll fix it up for you first thing."

Turns out he's handy. Fixes the door, dripping kitchen faucet, cleans out the woodstove, puts two mice traps back of the refrigerator so I don't hear that squeaking no more and that's just the start.

After I get kind of used to him coming round I ask him to sit for a cup of coffee after his chores is done. I go to open the kitchen cabinet to get two mugs and right off he sees my ribbons. I don't hold with showing them but Mama nailed them up in the cabinet one time when I was off to Sheridan. Twenty-seven and the greater part of them red.

"You ride them broncs?" Roberto asks me.

"In the long time past."

"Wow, I always wanted to learn how to do that," he says, tasting his coffee and putting the mug down. "What you put in this stuff?"

"Here's the sugar." I push it to him. He shovels in a bunch.

"You think I'm too old to learn?" he asks me.

"How old are you, son?"

"Twenty-seven last February. Been working four years for the IHS, best I could do around here."

"They keep you trotting?"

He takes a paper out of his jeans pocket. "Nineteen old folks. I got to see each and every one of them every single darned week."

"Not much time left for horses."

"Guess not, but you know what? Can I call you Cowboy? That's what they all call you."

"Just call me Jacob, the name I go by now."

"I guess when you get old..." He knows enough to stop.

"I stopped riding when my knees went," I tell him. "Sold my last horse a year ago. Not too long after that my last wife died."

"Seems like a lot all at once," Roberto says.

"You live long enough, you see it."

"Let's take a look at that linoleum. We want to fix anything might trip you up."

I show him the kitchen floor, don't let on I've already taken a tumble there.

He tries to flatten out the corner of that old linoleum so stiff broke off in his hand. "Looks like we're going to have to put you in a whole new floor."

"No need of that, son. Just shove that stool over it."

"Well for now." The stool covers up the broke-off piece but I know Roberto isn't one to be satisfied with make-dos. "I'm going to measure," he says. "Hold one end." There we are down on our knees with the tape measure stretched out between us and he's asking me what color I favor. I tell him green makes no difference to me.

He writes down the measurements and the color on his little pad then packs up his tools and goes off. By and by Ramona come to check what he's done. She sees the stool shoved over the broke piece. "Roberto measured for new but I don't see the need, cost a lot of money," I tell her.

"We honor our elders," Ramona says like one thing follows another.

I start to get the feeling I'm on some kind of treadmill, linoleum roll dropped at the door while I'm still pondering if I really do favor green. Roberto and a man name of Juan lay it down. Hammering most of one morning. Once they're done and satisfied I ask the two guys if they want coffee. Roberto warns against it.

"You boil some water I'll make tea," he says. I put the pot on. Roberto takes two little squibs out of his pocket. "Lemon Sour Grass Tea with Saffron."

"I never did hear of that," I say.

"Good for the immune system. You want to try some?"

Well I try it but it's weak as water, yellow water. "I'll stick to my coffee," I say.

Juan goes off on another job but Roberto keeps coming back regular with Ramona on his heels checking "the quality of his workmanship." I ask her one time what she thinks of the workmanship of this building but she says it's not her job to criticize the government.

It was winter when Mama Blacksleeves died and still a new year when Roberto, Ramona, and me met up and by spring we's all pretty good friends, good as I want anyway. I'm all the time trying to steer Ramona away from these big jobs like storm windows, seems like she has all the government money in the world to spend on me. Leave well enough alone is my motto but I never can get her to listen. Storm windows go up in February and I will say they keep the worst of the wind out.

Roberto's different, not that fond of work helped me two or three times to get clear of it. Did clean the leaves off the roof that opened up a leak. Leaves stopped it up just fine but once they was gone rainwater run down the wall behind my TV. Well that would not do and Ramona set Roberto to patching. He was up there trampling around and whistling by the time spring turned to summer.

In June he's obliged to come working on my roof in that early heat and I'm asking him in for water. We sit at the kitchen table and get to talking. I'm hungry so I clue him in how Mama Blacksleeves learnt to fix my bacon, super crisp just this side of burnt. Roberto gets pretty good at it after a few tries. He tells me he's taking little fat hen Ramona out on dates.

"What for?" I ask him.

"I aim to get married," he says, "raise some kids."

"Well I guess she's good as any."

"But she won't," he says. "She claims she's going to get out of here by fall go to the City make some real money."

"There'll be another one coming down the pike."

"I don't want no nother one, I want her."

"I got in that fix one time," I tell him. "Had terrible trouble getting out."

"Tell me about it, Mr. Jacob," he says. It's taken the better part of a year for him to call me that.

I lean way back in my mind. "I was close to your age, maybe a year younger, working on a crew building our juvie hall, we had government money."

"I did hear about that," he says.

"A big deal, a lot of work, ten or eleven of us boys on the job every day, foreman my cousin Tig hired me being family but didn't cut me no slack. We had the walls up good solid, putting the roof on, electrical and plumbing already in. Tig had the blueprints spread out on the hood of his truck the way he done every day. I took a short break seeing he was occupied went to find my bottle behind the Porta Potty. Well Tig must have seen me leaving and commenced to bawl at me. I answered back. I never have been one to stand chastising in front of a crowd. He come at me swinging. We was down in the dirt slugging it out and here come this pretty little girl bringing Tig's lunch in a basket covered with a checked cloth. When she seen us down in the dirt she commenced to scream, I jumped up ended it right then, never could stand a woman screaming. Tig was sore at me a couple of days then forgot about it. She never did."

Roberto was stirring sugar in his health tea. "What happened?"

"She started in calling me on the phone wanting to get together, 'process' what happened. I didn't see no sense in that and told her so. I needed the job and Tig would have fired me as quick as look at me if I fooled around with her. So what I'm trying to tell you, son, is leave Ramona alone for a week or so. She'll come looking for you just the way Tig's girl come looking for me."

"Not going to work, Mr. Jake. She knows I care."

"Not Jake, that name's taken permanent."

"Sorry...Mr. Jacob."

"She don't see you for a week maybe ten days she's going to come crawling."

"Is that what Tig's girl did?"

"You better believe it." I maybe should've stopped there but I had the bit in my teeth. "Got me in bed one Sunday afternoon told me right off she was going to break up with Tig."

"Not good," Roberto says.

"You bet not good. I worked on her but she was all stars and flowers, nothing was going to change her mind."

"So—?"

"Tig fired me just the way I knowed he would. I was so het up with all of it her being such a little fool and me a even bigger fool getting dragged into it I climbed up throwed a can of gasoline on the juvie hall roof burnt the place to the ground."

Roberto looks at me. "I heard you made some kind of trouble, never knew exactly what."

"Well now you know. Five years in the pen for arson and when I got back here there weren't a blade of work for me felon and so on. "

"Mr. Jacob you know you could've made it after you was in the pen."

"That's where you're wrong. Once they stick that orange jumpsuit on you you're cooked."

That's a long way around to the trouble he's having with Ramona and I tell him so. "Let her leave, son, if she wants to leave. She'll come back."

I guess me burning down juvie hall made some kind of a mark on Roberto's mind. He didn't do nothing to keep Ramona—she left pronto and sure enough seventeen months later she's back. Took longer than I estimated but so what. Roberto asked me to come to the wedding and I have a plan to do it if I can come up with something decent to wear.

We don't go in that much for weddings so I'm not real sure what I'm getting into but I put on my first store-bought suit and Christ that thing itches. It's hot, late

August, and smoke from the big fire up north clouding the sky. I taste all those pinion and juniper trees burning.

I don't drive now my eyes are failing, so it's a quandary how to get twenty-two miles to Sheridan. I used to hitch everywhere when my license was taken for this or that so it's natural to walk out to the highway and hold out my thumb. Guess drivers ain't so used nowadays to somebody hitching, particularly somebody old in a new suit. A lot fly on by but then this young lady in a blue electric car stops, window comes down she tells me to hop in.

Now this is the first that kind of car I've been in though many in the ads on TV. I settle in the front seat admire the screen she has in place of a dashboard, all kinds of lights and signals flashing. She pulls out at a good clip, says, "My name's Nancy."

"My name's Jacob not Jake. I never met up with no Nancy before."

"I'm from Chicago," she says like that makes sense of her name. "Drove all the way out here by myself seeing the sights."

"What sights?" I ask. She has the AC going full blast and I see her little foot in a black high-heeled shoe pressing down hard on the gas. She sure does drive fast.

"The parks, the reservations, I already been to a sweat lodge," she says proud as punch.

"Used to be we didn't do those for no outsiders."

"We need them bad as you do, Jacob," she says and I catch sight of her knee at the edge of her short skirt. Oh she is a looker and smells good too.

"What else you seen?" I ask her to keep the talk going.

"Stayed in a motel that was wigwams."

"You mean those concrete ones east of Helena?"

"Yes and the one I was in had these paintings all over the walls, ceremonials and things like that. Air-conditioned too. I stayed three days."

"We didn't have no real wigwams. That's down on the plains."

She looks at me like I just broke her heart. "Didn't your people live in them?"

"Not far as I know. It's all government housing now. You pass by here on your way back to Chicago I'll invite you in."

"I would love that!" She looks at me. "Where're you going now all dressed up with your thumb out?"

"Somebody I know getting hitched in Sheridan."

"Romantic!" She has a sigh in her voice.

"Well I don't know about that. This particular gal run off for seventeen months—he has to get hitched to get her back. Time he knows it's the wrong move, it'll be too late."

"Maybe he never will come to that conclusion," she says. She has the prettiest little mouth all screwed up painted like a rosebud and I wish I was young enough to do something foolish.

"I've got granddaughters about your age not nearly so pretty," I say, letting myself go that far.

She giggles, swerving around a truck going ninety. "Oh you're just talking," she says, making it back in line just in time. "I bet the girls are all over you."

"Not so much these days. You got a hubby back in the big city?"

"Not anymore," she says.

I know it's time to rein myself in, easier to do if she didn't have those little fingernails like pearls on the wheel. "Well you'll get another one soon enough," I say.

"Maybe out here." She throws me this smile.

"Not on your life, nothing but trouble around here. And don't be telling me you like trouble."

We go on that way, the old back-and-forth I thought was finished for good, till we're driving into Sheridan. It's Saturday traffic like I never expect to see. She turns on a voice tells her how to get to the church. I think she'll drop me in front where a lot of cars are gathering but she slides the electric into a space, parallel parking I've never known a woman to pull off.

"Can I come in with you, Jacob?" she asks with that smile would melt a iceberg.

I can't say no to this lady and it comes to me the bride and groom might get a kick out of seeing me with her, last thing they'd expect on the face of this earth.

We're coming in late the pews, all packed. I never knew Roberto or Ramona had so many kin and friends. Everybody all dressed up and I'm glad for my suit hot as it is. My little lady is all smiles like she's waited years for this particular occasion and I'm kind of pleased to be there too. Flower smell so strong it drowns out even her scent.

We squeeze in next to a old pair just as the organ starts in groaning and all heads turn to the door. Here they come, Ramona in her white bride dress streaming all across the floor and what looks to be her father, old white man buttoned up tight. He has her hand firm on his arm as they go on down the aisle to the altar where Roberto is waiting looking fit to bust in a new blue suit.

Old white man shoves Ramona's hand off his arm, steps aside like he's relieved. Roberto takes the freed-up hand and the two of them turn to the Navajo medicine man I know from way back. Seems strange to me he's in this white-people church but that's how it is. He sings a blessing, begins to drone on. I don't hear too well but I see Roberto and Ramona nodding and moving lips so I guess they're saying what the Navajo wants to hear. Next to me my little lady is chirping like a bird. Then it's all over—the organ roars and the two of them come smirking back down the aisle.

"That's the prettiest thing I ever saw," Nancy says, "what a dress!" It's sweeping by us.

"You'll buy one even prettier," I tell her. She has tears in her eyes.

"Oh I'm just so glad I got to witness! Thank you, Jacob!"

"They'll have some food I guess. You want to eat?"

"You think it's all right, me being a stranger?"

"No strangers at this kind of thing if I remember rightly."

She clamps her hand in the crook of my arm and I see those little pearl fingernails shining. They have a scratch in them too. We sashay on out with everybody else and sure enough they have tables set out under the trees. Every kind of good food and plenty of wine and whiskey, I guess Ramona's daddy has means.

Quite a few folks I know from up on the rez and Nancy wants to meet every one of them. The old ladies get to staring and whispering and I know they'll have something to chew on for days, me with this pretty white girl must be thirty years younger. One old lady gives me the stink-eye and I know she's mad 'cause I never have gone out with any of her kind. Never will either, doing fine on my own.

My little lady pushes right up to Ramona, gives her a big kiss. Reaches out to shake with Roberto and he's looking at her like he'd sure love to get closer. I don't have no reason to be proud but proud I am. Roberto pulls me to one side, says, "Where'd you find her, Jacob?"

"Hitching to get here," I say. "She picked me up in one of them electric cars."

"Well you hang on to her," he says with a grin I don't like at all.

"She's on her way back to Chicago," I tell him but he just snuffles up a laugh like he sure knows better.

She fills up two plates at the long table, chicken beef corn tostadas all the fixings. We go sit on the ground under a tree. She helps me down and I know I need it, knees creaking like rusty door hinges. She's got a big appetite for somebody so small, even goes back for seconds, takes my plate without me saying a word, fills it up too. I can't eat all that. She got down all of hers. Then it's a hunt for the bathroom.

We find it and take turns like proper. Coming out I see Roberto and Ramona getting ready to take off. Their truck is pulled up in front of the church and folks are throwing rice and yelling. The two of them duck in the truck and drive off rattling cans tied on the bumper.

My little lady is waving. "Oh this is so romantic!" she tells me. I know we best be leaving before she gets any more worked up. She don't want to leave but I tell her I got business at home, have to get back. So we make it to the electric car and she jumps in behind the wheel still going on about how romantic.

The whole way back she's singing those old-time radio tunes, "Red Sails in the Sunset," "Tea for Two" and so on. She has a pretty high voice with all the quavers in the right place and I know some guy is going to like listening for a while then tell her shut the hell up. Them high lady voices can be tiring.

She pulls up in front of my place, looks at me waiting for me to ask her in. I ain't learned much in my life but I have learned enough to know where such foolishness leads. "I thank you for picking me up and going with me," I say, my hand on the door.

"You want me to drive off and just leave you?" she says, going all pitiful. "We just shared an important experience."

"Yes we did," I say, "but it's late and I'm tired. I'm old, Nancy."

"You don't seem all that old to me," she says, pouting up that pretty mouth.

"You see the white hair on my chest and my old-man belly you'd think different. I don't go with women these days."

"I guess you miss your wife."

I let that go. Mama and I quit all that by general agreement five years before she passed, just no more appetite.

I open the door. "Goodbye, Nancy. Hit the thruway now you'll have a couple hours daylight driving."

She reaches out, lays her little pearl-nailed fingers on my arm. "I won't forget you, Jacob."

"It's sure I won't forget you." I crawl out, slam the door.

It's a minute or more before she starts the engine. She pulls out, grinding on the gravel and spurring that electric car. I hear her wheels screech around the corner and it's like I see her whole life rolling out: love husbands disappointments divorces maybe three or four kids growing up running wild. That's the way things go now and it makes me real tired just thinking about it.

Inside I smell the bacon I fried for breakfast, see the smoke from it burning still hanging in the close indoor air. I go to open the window and pushing it up I feel something in my right arm. Just a twitch or a pinch like I need reminding.

Then it's quiet light fading fast. I turn on the TV get my blanket wrap myself up and lay down.

THE LAST OF THE LAST

I don't care for news but it seems like it cares for me and always comes at me some way so I did hear the dudes up in Washington was saying they was going to close down our old folks' home because they weren't enough of us in it. Most of the old I know say dying in a ditch a better way to go and not that many old anymore anyway. A lot went during the Covid.

Uncle Joe'd been in the home quite a while wasn't anywhere else for him to go. Family long gone except my daughter Bonnie Blue. She come by one afternoon early in the winter and went to working on me and I let her.

"Now you know, Daddy, you can't go on here like this," she said like anybody cared what I ate, mostly bologna, or what I did with my trash, stored in the closet till it started to stink. Nobody cared till now but now there was a reason. "You always said Uncle Joe was your kind of old and now we need you to go on in there so he has company and you can help us keep the home open."

"Uncle Joe don't know me from a hole in the wall," I told her. "Last time I went to see him he just went on staring at his two hands fiddling in his lap."

"And you run off the road on the way home, hit that tree, busted your windshield and your nose. You know they's going to take your keys any day now."

I saw then she had me pitched in a corner and wished I didn't like her so much, cute and round in those skin-tight pants they all wear winter or no winter. She was always one of the best of mine as far as I'm concerned.

The long and the short of it was my grandson Sam-the-Man and his wife Jo Ann come packed up everything took my keys drove me up to the home and I didn't find a word to say against it. They'd quit saving my place at the True West, eyes not working so good in the dark, and now they took my keys I wouldn't be going nowhere for company. And I do like company. Beer don't taste so good no more, appetite just about gone, but sitting around chewing the fat with some others of us still a lot better than every night switching channels on the TV.

Me packed in the back seat Sam riding shotgun Jo Ann driving like she always done, and fast. She pulled up next to the home with dark just gathering, the moon sloping toward full and a few stars blinking. Cold but that's winter for you.

Not too many words between the three of us, we all knew what we was doing and no way back.

Bonnie Blue must have called made the arrangements—the place is free for tribal members so she didn't have to arrange much. Soon as we pulled up these two nursies or whatever they was, no uniforms so it's hard to tell, come racing with a wheelchair, tried to push me in it.

"He'll walk," Sam said, just about his first words.

"Well no we have to wheel him, liability, insurance blah blah blah." So they pushed me in the chair tucked a blanket tight around me hot as it was when we got in that place. They must have a furnace big as a mountain going full blast.

Up in the elevator all kinds of chat I didn't pay it no mind. Jo Ann making nice, that was enough, Sam silent as the grave. I wondered did he mind what they was doing.

Rolled down the second-floor hall, they knocked on Uncle Joe's door—well it was open so knocked on the edge out of respect I guess. Poor old guy sitting in his wheelchair looking out the window at our mountains. I wondered don't he ever get out of that chair? Some kind of gown knotted up around him, skinny bare legs but real shoes on his feet (no socks) so I guessed he did walk some.

"You got company Joe," one of them nursies hollered and I guessed Joe done gone deaf since he been there.

"Company that's planning to stay!" the other nursie shouted like he should be glad.

Old man turned his head slow on his skinny chicken neck looked at me like he didn't know who the hell I was.

One of them thumped my wheelchair right up next to his, Jo Ann saying, "You know him it's your old friend Cowboy."

"Jacob now," I said, climbed out of that chair before anybody could get started about liability and got right up in Joe's face. "We's going to be roommates till death do us part, old fart," I said.

He turned those milky old-age eyes on me but after a while they was a spark at the bottom of the left one and he held out his plain old shaking hand. It was warm and I grabbed it hard, remembered how he always held his reins kind of loose with some power that horses seemed to get and paid mind. Never was one to jerk and saw.

Jo Ann was shoving my stuff in the closets and drawers and I saw there wasn't much of anything in there and got why Joe was wearing that raggedy gown. Daughter run off years ago, son died, young grandchildren throwed to the winds so when they come to take him to the home they was nothing much left to go with him. I told Jo Ann to buy him some stuff. I had everything I needed but nothing to spare.

There was some more hemming and hawing, Jo Ann making a fuss about how nice the room was, clean linoleum on the floor with blue flowers in it, sink in the corner, a little towel hung on a hook and some kind of a rolling pisser right between the two beds. "Look at them good thick blankets—I don't have nothing like that at home!" and so on, Joe looking at me now like he could eat me. We always been pals rode the circuit together sat in every bar in every town in the West. Well that built memories just like what kitchen tables and baby bottles and some girl's panties slung on a chair do.

It seemed to me like high time for all of them to clear out but Jo Ann laid down the law, said they'd wait till the supper trays come. Well they feed the animals early in the zoo so here the carts come rattling before the sun had set. Some more shouting but I guess Joe being stone deaf now it was called for or maybe just what they did.

Taking covers off hot dishes, looked pretty good, some kind of meat two veggies a big wad of chocolate cake. Would have been a feast for me when I was home more or less taking care of myself.

One of the nursies said to me, "He never do eat but you get started give him the example."

So I plowed into that meat with the plastic knife and fork, Joe sat there watching like he never seen a man chew. I reached over to his tray, cut up his meat fine, speared a piece on a fork, held it close to his mouth. He opened up like a baby bird and I shoved it in. Jo Ann went to clapping and nursies just overall delighted.

By cake time Jo Ann and Sam-the-Man said nighty-night and the nursies went off too. There we sat, two old men one feeding the other. Joe ate everything on his plate 'cept the squash. I speared a piece held it to his mouth, he turned his head away sharp like I was trying to poison him. I recollected he never had cared much for squash, maybe didn't like the color yellow.

One guy some kind of orderly come pretty quick to take the trays said it was time to get in bed. "Leave us do our business," I told him. "I'll potty him wash him up get him in his bed cut out the light." It took some back-and-forth but finally this guy said OK, guessed I wasn't going to let our privacy go just because we was old.

Joe was limp as a empty sack so I nearly sprung my back hoisting him out of that chair. I was puffing. "Put your hands on the handles and push!" Well I guess he did and it was some kind of little help.

I got him out and on the pisser, he did what he needed I thought I probably going to have to get him up in the night do it again, the night looking to be long when it started so early. I washed what I could of him with a cloth wrung out in warm water, dried him with that little towel, put the old worn-out PJs on him and would you know he started singing in this cracked old voice would have scared the ravens.

"Rock of ages, cleft for me."

Sung that line over and over, I guess had forgot the

rest. I chipped in "Low we bow the adoring knee," tried to remember more, took his toothbrush and went as deep in his mouth as he'd let me, rinsed with warm water that dribbled down his front. That little small towel soaked from earlier, so I took one of my T-shirts out the drawer and dried him still trying to remember.

I didn't, just them two lines.

Put him in, drawed the covers up to his chin. He reached out grabbed my arm saying something like, "Don't go."

"I'm not going anywhere, I'm here to stay," I told him and he settled back down.

I did my own cleanup, put on a fresh T-shirt and jockeys, never did care for those sissy pajamas. Didn't have no toothbrush, never have, teeth hard as rocks all my life. Slid in the other bed reached for the light pulled the chain, Joe still mumbling "Rock of ages..." Quieted down after a while and we both went to sleep and snoring.

He started whining late in the night and I got him up put him on the pisser, no soaked PJs while I was on duty. Remembered one woman or another getting up to feed and change dark of night whichever one was new or old. Well I was doing it now.

So it started and went on. Nursie Lisa the pretty one paid us special attention, even hung a string of lights on Joe's bed to mark Christmas, let me take him to the shower when it was time on Friday and roll him to the TV room but he don't pay it no mind, just cawed at me to take him back to our room.

Them days of winter was long. Joe never much on talk and less now so I come up with two old raggedy books from what they called the library—a shelf behind the nursie station—read him two real long ones before February. "The best of times and the worst of times" being one and "It is a far better thing I do now" the other. Didn't make a whole lot of sense to me, Joe just nodding and drowsing but it sure passed the time.

Pretty soon it got to where they was cutting corners, food not so good as that first meal, just mainly oatmeal sweet potatoes canned peaches kinda thing. Government done quit on tribal funding, said let the state do it and it don't.

Lisa let me go out in they little yard every now and then to smoke but Joe started crying when I went so I cut it down as much as I could. I don't know who that old man thought I was but he sure as hell wasn't going to let me go. I appreciated that. Seemed to me looking back everybody I depended on skedaddled soon as they could or sooner, dying early, running off parts unknown. Well not this time.

I got to liking Nursie Lisa but never did learn the names of the ones living in there except this old lady Bertha, took some kind of a liking to me, made a nuisance of herself coming in our room till Joe started to shout at her and she went. He did have words when they was needed but mainly just croaked them old hymns we learned in the Jesuit boarding school before time got started.

Him hardly eating at all unless it was them canned peaches, doctor come after a while said his heart was going. I guess Joe heard him 'cause he started in again on "Rock of Ages" so loud I thought his heart was going to stop then and there but it didn't.

March that last late snow Joe started to try to tell me what he wanted. It took me a while to figure out his broke-up words and finally I knew he was saying, "Out out get me out" or something of the kind.

When Jo Ann come to visit—she come pretty regular once a month, Sam-the-Man never—I told her Joe wanted out, she just smiled shook her head. Nowhere for him to go or me neither. By then they'd sold my house. Joe never had one, camped with some daughter or other those last years, them ladies all gone.

No use trying to say all this to Joe, he never did put much faith in words even when we was young and they maybe mattered more. He went to moaning and carrying on every time the sun was setting and even them old hymns didn't do him no good so I started looking for a way out.

They had us pretty well locked in there and from the noises I heard just about every night they was more than one wanted out. Every now and then I'd hear one of them male nursies pounding down the hall after somebody in a wheelchair trying to get away. Some of them could wheel pretty fast.

Second week of March, Lisa more or less give me the run of the place. I started looking around found this back door on the ground floor they sometimes forgot to lock after the garbage was hauled out. It went out on Wednesdays and when the next Wednesday come around I told Joe we was going and he clapped them frail old hands like he understood every word, maybe he did.

I got him in his chair after the guy come for our supper trays and things got quiet with lights out. Rolled him out in the hall got to the elevator, nobody around, they thought we was all gone to sleep. Rode down and rolled out on the ground floor, went the back way I knew of past the storerooms, not nobody there that time of night, to that door I knew about. Sure enough it was not locked.

They used to call me that long time ago: Sure Enough.

Some kind of luck.

I rolled Joe on out into the dark still night and he commenced to bawl that old hymn. We was out beyond the light shed by the home and I never felt the need to shut him up.

I put in "Low we bow the adoring knee" though far as I knowed our knees old and creaky as they was couldn't do nothing about bowing.

No use rolling down the road, somebody bound to see us drive us back. We parked.

New moon blew up over our mountains sailing on the clouds that come and went, snow before morning, that fresh smell in the air. Joe went to whimpering so I tucked the blanket tight around him and it seemed to work for a while.

Arroyo off to the left leading down into dark trees. I saw a more or less path and started his chair down creaking and bumping over stones, Joe don't say a thing. I knowed them arroyos since I was little, they sink and sink sometimes it seems like they reach to the bottom of the world, this one was sure deep, that path give out before the bottom. I pushed Joe on through the tore-up roots of them tough old pinions laid bare by the floods, earth showing its changes. Finally come to a stop, a bare place more or less level, might have been the bottom.

"Well here we are," I told Joe, stopped his chair, put on the brakes and sat down next him on the ground. It was froze pretty solid and I raked some leaves over it for comfort, made me some kind of nest.

He was quiet. I guess after a little he went to sleep.

New moon rising over the top of the arroyo too little to shed much light. I didn't have no coat, put my hands between my knees pressed hard to warm them, it helped some. Clouds closing in, it was dark.

Toward midnight the cold settled in steady and Joe was quiet in his chair.

I stayed eyes open beside him till maybe the first hours of the morning, then I laid myself down on the leaves and shuffled them up around me.

Snow starting to fall those last dark hours, I felt a few flakes land on my face and reared up to look at Joe, snow covering him little by little, he was still.

Laid down in the leaves beside him took one look at the little new moon riding high over our mountains. Closed my eyes.

LAYING COWBOY DOWN

Once the ground thawed in May, Sam and Jo Ann took Cowboy out of cold storage in his bag—he died in March—and hauled him in the back of Sam's truck to the funeral home that had popped up overnight next to the gas station on the south edge of town. Cowboy'd been froze pretty solid and stayed froze.

"I wish you'd let me help you chose his coffin," Jo Ann said, getting in the truck. It was Saturday afternoon and she had on what she called her leisure clothes, shorts too short and top too tight but Sam had give up on saying anything. She did what she did.

"You'd've made me buy the highest price one they had," he said, starting the truck.

"Well something better than a plain wood box anyway." Sam had made the mistake of taking a shot of the coffin with his cell phone and sending it to her. "I'd have planted him in that settee he made, said it'd serve for his coffin," Jo Ann told him.

"Them Colorado folks bought his house furnished."

"Being who he was, Cowboy deserved better."

"You tell me who he was," Sam said, pulling into the parking lot by the low cement building with the sign "Franklin Family Funeral Home We Care."

"He made you what you are for one thing," Jo Ann said. "Cured you of the I-don't-cares some way."

"He was after you from the day he set eyes on you," Sam said. "Used to call you Big Boobs."

"I thought he was kind of sweet, old as he was."

"Old and goat randy. Some of them old ones never do grow out of it."

"He always treated me with respect," Jo Ann said, and Sam knew they needed to get out of the truck fast or start something they'd have trouble stopping. He knew she'd have a whole lot less piss and vinegar if she was seven months gone and with a one-year-old heavy in her arms. He'd quit on that, too.

They walked into the sudden cool in the funeral parlor and a tall white man in a black suit come sticking out his hand. He had one of them long white-men faces seems all jaw with the hair combed smooth on top of his head. He gave his name and shook Jo Ann's hand and went to give her a hug but she turned her shoulder to him. Then he shook Sam's hand but he was still looking at Jo Ann. "Glad to see you both come to make the final arrangements."

"We come to pick up the coffin is all," Sam said, hoping to cut him off at the gap.

"I'll have Juan bring it to your conveyance," the man said, turning to shout for Juan somewhere in the back.

Sam wished he'd listened to the man's name. Easier to talk to him if he called him by name.

Here came Juan and Sam gaped. It was his half brother Mike wearing some kind of work uniform and grinning like the devil.

"Hello, bro," he said to Sam, and ducked his head to Jo Ann.

"His name's Mike," Sam said to the man in the suit.

He smiled. "A lot of our clients are Spanish speakers. We try to make them comfortable."

"Spanish speakers can say Mike."

Jo Ann was making a face at him. "Let's go see to the coffin."

Juan/Mike went off through another door. Sam and Jo Ann headed out through the main entrance, the man in the suit coming behind. They waited a few minutes in the driveway and the man in the suit filled the gap by asking if they wanted to make a date for a Celebration of Life and Jo Ann said before Sam could, "Thank you but we're going to do that back home."

The man wished them closure to their grief and went

back inside. A minute later Juan/Mike come rolling the coffin on a set of wheels and the three of them hoisted it onto the truck bed next to Cowboy in his bag.

"How come you let him give you a new name?" Sam asked Juan/Mike.

"Only job I could get coming out of jail," Juan/Mike said. "Be obliged if you don't spread it back home."

"Of course we won't," Jo Ann said and hustled into the truck, setting herself in the driver's seat and waving her hand out the window for the keys.

"What they pay you?" Sam asked his half brother.

"Minimum but they let me live in the back room here. Coffee maker, hot plate, microwave. Works pretty good for me. I wash in the big sink they use to clean up the bodies, pee in the bushes, go up the road to the gas station for the other. Pretty good far as I see it."

Sam pulled out a pack of cigarettes and held it out. Juan/Mike took one. "You wash them corpses?"

Jo Ann stopped waving her hand out the window.

"They got a team comes in when they call. Blood and all that. I ain't qualified."

Sam leaned on the tailgate, drew in a lungful of smoke, let it out and laughed. "Bro, I don't know what you is qualified for but I'm glad it's not cleaning corpses."

"I do just about everything else," Juan/Mike said like his feelings was hurt.

Jo Ann tooted the horn.

"Well, we got to get Cowboy in that coffin and in the ground before he melts," Sam said, stubbing his cigarette out under his boot. "See you around. You coming up for the Easter dances?"

"If they give me time off."

Sam gave his half brother a good knock on the shoulder and went to get in the truck shotgun and Jo Ann pulled out like they was being chased.

"We got to stop by home for shovels," Sam said.

"You going to bury him right off? Nobody but the two of us?"

"Two's a crowd," Sam said. "I'm planning something at the dances to send him off."

"Well that's news to me," Jo Ann said.

They drove on without saying another word. Sam knew that was a mercy. Jo Ann was flushed to the edge of her hair which was not a good sign. She never could understand why he never talked about his plans. She called it sharing which was not something Sam did.

At home she pulled up to the double-wide and sat while Sam went to the shed for the shovels.

He carried them out, threw them in the back of the truck. "Let's get going. Watch your speed. You already got one ticket to pay off."

"I don't aim to do a thing about that till they make me," she said with that head toss that always made Sam smile. She had a full head of black hair more or less natural and when she threw her head it spread out like a wing.

"Well don't come whining to me when they shut you up in jail."

She threw her hair again. "They don't jail folks for not paying a ticket."

She pulled around the corner, wheels squealing, out to the field where they'd just finished putting up a white wood fence around the graveyard. Sam jumped out to open the gate and bowed her through and saw her big smile flashing out at him. She had to stop for him to lead the way. No burial of theirs since Mama Blacksleeves and that was a long time before.

Walking, it amazed Sam to see fake flowers on the graves. He thought only Mexicans did that.

He waved Jo Ann to stop by their graves, marked with wooden crosses already washed bare of names and dates but he knew it was Mama Blacksleeves and the great-great-grandma run off before he was born but come back home to die and be put in their piece of earth. A few of the family men from old times whose names he sort of knew but nothing for quite a while because now they died all over the place and were buried wherever they fell.

Jo Ann got out of the truck and they let down the tailgate and slid Cowboy out. The bag looked too white to go into the dirt. Sam walked off six feet from Mama

Blacksleeves's cross and handed Jo Ann one shovel and started to dig with the other. No rain since Christmas and the dirt was about as hard as cement but he turned up an edge, left that for Jo Ann, went to the other side and turned up an edge there. She was a hard worker, he had to say that, kept pace with him digging, inch by inch and foot by foot. They was sweating and the sun was stinging the sweat on their faces and they stopped at three feet to swig out of the Pepsi that Jo Ann had thought to bring along. The fizzy water was warm but it hit the spot and they wiped the sweat off their faces and got down in the hole and commenced to dig again.

"Should of brought gloves," Jo Ann said and showed Sam three blisters at the roots of her right three fingers.

"Another two feet," he told her. "Dirt's easier here." It broke away from their shovels in dark brown clots, damp from being so far down.

"That's six feet," he said, huffing and crawled up out of the hole. Jo Ann crawled up the other side, her bare knees brown with dirt.

"Help me slide him in the coffin," Sam said.

"You got to unscrew the lid first."

Sam went into his truck for his screwdriver. Whoever'd screwed on the top had done it like it was supposed to hold for all eternity and he had to work hard undoing all the screws. He pocketed them. "Come on," he told Jo Ann.

She was standing there crying. "It's like I'm counting on seeing him again at the dances," she said, "like he's always going to be there, sitting on the ledge outside the church."

"Well he's going to be there in some shape even if we can't see him," Sam said. "You know he wouldn't miss it."

She wiped her eyes with the back of her hand. "I hate to look at that bag, too white for him seems like to me. Couldn't you find no other color like red he'd have liked?"

"No," Sam said. He was glad he didn't see Cowboy before some man at the old folks' home shoved him in the bag and locked him up in their freezer.

"Well, what'd you give them to put on him?" She said like it was some kind of consolation.

"His regalia. He told me a long time ago that's what he wanted."

"All of it?"

"Every bit. Kilt, foxtail, earrings, bracelets, leggings, that big turquoise and silver necklace he always wore."

"That's good money buried in the ground."

"It's what he wanted," Sam said. "Toward the end he started going back to the old ways, asked me to put him up on the scaffold but I told him don't nobody do that now."

"Well let's slide off the top and get him in."

They slid the top off. A big raven settled in the pinion at the side of the graveyard and commenced to squawking. "Telling Cowboy goodbye," Sam said.

That did it. Jo Ann crouched down by the coffin and started in crying again.

"Never knew you cared so much about him," Sam said.

"Oh he was a devil but I knew his heart was good," she said, her voice rumpled by sobs.

"He wouldn't want to see you down in the dirt crying," Sam told her and she got up and swiped the tears off her face again. Sam reached for the bag and took the end of it and felt the big bunched shoulder muscles and remembered Cowboy on his last horse, that dang mustang, give him all kinds of trouble.

"Get his feet," he told Jo Ann and she grabbed the other end of the bag and they dropped him in the coffin. They'd seasoned him up well at the funeral place and there was only a little stink of chemicals and he was still froze solid.

Sam got the lid on and started screwing it down.

Then they heaved and pulled and got the coffin to the edge of the hole. Sam didn't want to just drop Cowboy down. He got some rope from his truck and strung it under the coffin and give one end to Jo Ann and told her to go to the other side of the hole. He held onto the other end. Then he teetered the coffin on the edge of the hole and when it started to slide, he hollered, "Hold on!" It looked like Jo Ann was going to get pulled in but then she set her boots and strained on the rope and between them they lowered it down. A little bumpy and it landed crooked.

Sam pulled on his rope and got the coffin straight. Then he told Jo Ann to let go of her end and pulled the rope out. "Now we're going to fill it," he said.

"Wait a minute." She went to a next-door grave, not theirs, and pulled up some fake yellow flowers and threw them in on top of the coffin before Sam could say anything.

"He always hated them fake flowers," he told her.

"He liked yellow."

"Get started," he said. They went to prying with their shovels at the mounds of loose dirt they'd dug out of the hole. Dropped it on the coffin lid and just about had it covered when Hank come rattling in his pickup.

"What in hell you kids doing?" he shouted, sliding out.

"Burying Cowboy," Sam said.

"You going to do that without me? What the hell!" Hank shouted. "Ain't I his oldest great-grandson?"

"We just wanted to spare you the grief," Jo Ann said.

Hank went round the hole and grabbed her shovel out of her hands. He commenced shoveling in big wads of dirt and in two minutes the coffin was covered. He jumped in and stamped the loose dirt down with his boots, stamping more than was called for.

"Where's the marker?" he asked Sam, toning down a little.

"We ordered it but it ain't come yet."

"Well you can't leave him bare." He started feeling in his pants pocket and come up with his enamel lighter, blue as a bluebird's wing, squatted down, made a hole in the dirt and pushed the lighter in so only the top part showed. He patted the dirt around it. "Old man sure did love his smokes."

Jo Ann said, "That's what killed him."

"Not the way I heard it. Froze to death in that arroyo with Uncle Joe."

Jo Ann edged away from him. He went off to the sickly aspen somebody had planted to mark another set of graves. It was just leafing out. Went in back of it and started to grunt and sob and say, "Great-Grandpa, oh Great-Grandpa." He come out zipping his fly. "Call of nature," he said and lurched on to his pickup, crawled in and flew off.

"Well I guess that's it," Jo Ann said. "Seems strange to just leave him."

Sam bowed over the grave and said the one sentence he recollected from some prayer. "In the valley of the shadow of death...In the valley of the shadow of death."

And then they left him. That was it until the dances.

A while back Sam had learned from one of the elders he wasn't to dance till he'd done a purification, nothing personal, just the way men always did when they'd been in jail didn't matter what for. In his case it was next to nothing, a little piece of burning he'd needed to do to get rid of some past he wasn't planning on keeping. He knew better than to argue and he didn't have the time right then for the purification so he didn't dance for a while.

"You got to dance this time for Cowboy," Jo Ann told him after they buried the old man. "You know he expects it."

Sam did know that and also knew he didn't appreciate being reminded. He went to Old Man Salty, Cowboy's nephew, the only one left now from those seven brothers and one sister that had tore things up for a while. He asked him what he had to do.

Salty was sitting in his big old wing chair where he spent most days, now crippled up from too many horse accidents. He'd been a bull rider way too long into his late years, thrown rolled stamped and pawed till it was a wonder he was still alive. One of them bulls even bit him in the nose which they was not known to do.

"You got to go up to the top of Baldy," Salty told him. That was the tallest mountain in their range. "You got to spend thirty-six hours alone up there."

It was still getting down below freezing at night. "Can I take a tent?"

"Nothing but one blanket," Salty said.

"Food?"

"No food. One canteen of water."

Sam knew Jo Ann would never give him any peace

till he did it. They'd been married for three years and she acted like she owned him which was sometimes all right and sometimes not. She also had a loudmouth mama and three old aunties and Sam knew he wouldn't have a chance of getting out of the purification with that bunch.

Jo Ann sweetened up considerable in the days before he went, found him a thermal blanket and a good-size canteen. He couldn't see how far her sweetness would carry them before he left because the purification rules extended a week before and a week after but he planned to remind her when the time come that she did owe him.

He had a fierce climb getting up to the top of Baldy and there was snow up there which he hadn't expected. He scraped a patch bare and laid his blanket down and stood the canteen beside it. Then there was nothing to do but wait till dark and it took a long time coming.

Sitting on the blanket, Sam watched the sun slink down over the western range. The sky turned pink and yellow around the orange sun and Sam wondered why he'd never noticed that before. Likely it did that every evening at least in clear weather. Then a sparkler star come out and shone bright till the moon rose and blotted it. The moon was full or almost, a slice out of one edge, and Sam thought it might be a good sign that he was doing his purification in its bright cold light.

He set himself to thinking what it was he was trying to get rid of that'd stuck to him after jail down in

Helena. It wasn't his first time there and he suspicioned it wouldn't be his last and he'd handled it just the way he had before and would again. First night he'd shouted to them boys in the row of next-door cells: "You seen any white boys in here? How come everybody's brown or black?" That way they knew he was a fighter and the ones that wanted to mess with him left him alone except for the big black queen called hisself "Your Mama" but that was OK by Sam.

He thought maybe that was what he was supposed to get purified of. He was no Two Spirits and acting like one for a little bit maybe seemed like a sin. Not knowing exactly what to do he clawed up handfuls of dirt and rubbed his face and neck, lifted up his shirt and rubbed his belly too. That felt like the right way to go, half-frozen earth from the top of Baldy. Then he was shivering and got up and started pacing around in a circle chanting some words he remembered in the old language nobody talked anymore. Last one talked that way was Great-Aunt Cleome and she only started when she was so old she was half crazy. Talk of teaching it down at the school but Sam knew that was never going nowhere.

Full dark come on, coyotes howling down in the valley, Sam paced faster till he was running, panting, had to sit down. Looked out into the long darkness wondered where Cowboy and all the other dead had got to, was they around somewhere in the thin cold air. Huddled his blanket up around him but it didn't do no good he was cold to the bone and stood up again and commenced jumping. Jumped and shouted till his voice give out, sat down again drank a little water, tin-tasting from the old canteen Jo Ann dug up somewhere. Why not one of them plastic thermoses but then he knew that wouldn't go, tin canteen from the old days of riding and herding before all the young ones went off somewhere for this and that and the old ones went to dying.

Tired cold stared out into the darkness, saw the way it was built layers one on the other, started sorting through the layers with his eyes, coyotes closer now. Might come snuffling round see if he brung some food, wished he had his pistol but not allowed for sure. Remembered that big black queen saying "Come to your Mama," how good it sounded him having no mama he could recall. Stared out into those layers again, saw his face staring back at him, knew it couldn't be regular darkness, shut his eyes, opened again, there his face was. What in the name of Hell. His eyes looking into his eyes saying "Boy you want to be free you got to get rid all happened to you back then, do it with your blood." Had his pocketknife out soon as think of it, cut a slice out of his arm blood like a waterfall soaking in that dry earth. Wrapped his arm tight in the blanket blood soaked through. Laid on his arm all night to stop the bleeding got up in the morning saw the place where he'd laid soaked black, started back down the mountain calling singing crying. Sun coming up all gold Jo Ann at the bottom holding out a big cup of hot coffee.

"You done it," she said. "You done it, now you can dance for Cowboy." She bandaged up his arm soon as they got back to the house. Would have done more but for the purification rules.

And so Sam danced. Full regalia, one of the elders painted the white stripe from his forehead to his chin, Jo Ann watching with the rest of the women the drums going old men chanting everybody he knowed kids to elders dressed up pacing to the beat. Went on morning to sundown, little kids squatting down too tired, old men stooping leaning hands on knees then all started up again the drums never stopping. Sam sweating in the cold clear air smelling the sweat of all the kinfolk close around him wanting to reach out hold them till it was all over, darkness come down and quiet.

Jo Ann come to claim him. "Cowboy was there," she told him. "Sitting on the ledge outside the church the way he always done." Sam never did see him.

That night they had themselves a private party best they could do long as the purification rules lasted. Sam knew the real party was coming later.

ABOUT THE AUTHOR

Sallie Bingham is the author of eighteen books, including *Taken by the Shawnee, Little Brother: A Memoir, Treason: A Sallie Bingham Reader, The Silver Swan: In Search of Doris Duke*, and *Passion and Prejudice: A Family Memoir.* She is winner of the Thomas Wolfe Fiction Prize, *Foreword Magazine*'s Gold Medal in Fiction for *Mending: New & Selected Short Stories*, and her work has been included in *Best American Short Stories and the PEN/O. Henry Prize Stories*. She has received fellowships from Yaddo, MacDowell, and the Virgina Center for the Creative Arts. Bingham is founder of the Kentucky Foundation for Women and The Sallie Bingham Center for Women's History at Duke University. She was publisher of *The American Voice* from 1989 to 1998 and book editor at *The Courier Journal* from 1983 to 1989. She lives in Santa Fe.